## 'Are we decided, then, Rachel?'

David glanced at her almost as if he was reading her thoughts. 'That we try to achieve a friendlier environment?' He smiled, and there was a glint in his eyes that made Rachel catch her breath.

'Certainly,' she replied firmly. 'On condition that is how it remains, a friendly environment purely for working purposes.'

'If that's how you want it. . .'

'Yes, David,' she said crisply, 'that's how I want it.'

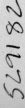

**Dear Reader**

NEVER PAST LOVING is Book Two of Margaret O'Neill's quartet, which has more of an administrative setting, and we launch the first of two books by Marion Lennox. A LOVING LEGACY involves general practice in outback Australia; you'll love Richard and Kate's battles. Next month, Richard's sister Christy will be our heroine. FALSE IMPRESSIONS by Laura MacDonald explores occupational nursing, and Margaret Barker returns to Ceres Island again, first met in her OLYMPIC SURGEON several years ago. This time, in SURGEON'S DILEMMA, Nicole's cousin Pippa is the heroine. Happy New Year!

*The Editor*

**Laura MacDonald** lives in the Isle of Wight. She is married and has a grown-up family. She has enjoyed writing fiction since she was a child, but for several years she has worked for members of the medical professional both in pharmacy and in general practice. Her daughter is a nurse and has also helped with the research for Laura's Medical Romances.

**Recent titles by the same author:**

SOMEBODY TO LOVE
A CASE OF MAKE-BELIEVE

# FALSE IMPRESSIONS

BY
LAURA MACDONALD

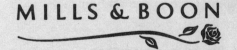

MILLS & BOON LIMITED
ETON HOUSE, 18–24 PARADISE ROAD
RICHMOND, SURREY, TW9 1SR

First published in Great Britain 1994
by Mills & Boon Limited

© Laura MacDonald 1994

Australian copyright 1994
Philippine copyright 1994
This edition 1994

ISBN 0 263 78440 1

Set in 10½ on 12½ pt Linotron Times
03-9401-46044

Typeset in Great Britain by Centracet, Cambridge
Made and printed in Great Britain

# CHAPTER ONE

THE injuries in the aftermath of the bomb explosion looked horrific. Flesh wounds caused by jagged pieces of metal gaped open and in some cases limbs had been severed. There was blood everywhere, drenching the clothes of the victims, seeping on to the floor and spattering the factory walls. The emergency services were stretched to their limits, the factory fire crew, ambulance and medical team being first on the scene only moments after the explosion, with the county services arriving soon afterwards. Five people had been killed, thirty seriously injured and a further twenty-two slightly injured. Some injuries had apparently been caused by the explosion dislodging flooring and equipment on the overhead jigs which had crashed on to the men working on the shop-floor. There had been no bomb warning so consequently no evacuation of the factory had been possible.

'Very realistic.'

Rachel Stevens blinked as Ron Banks, the health and safety officer, flicked the switch of the video recorder and someone at the back of the room turned on the light.

Together with other members of the medical team and the accident prevention team, Rachel had been

watching the video of a recent casualty faking that
they had staged at OBEX Aircraft Corporation.
This was the first time they had dealt with a potential
bombing, as in the past their fakings had centred on
air crashes and accident situations on the jigs or the
shop-floor.

'As usual we're looking for areas of improve-
ment,' said Ron. 'Does anyone have any immediate
thoughts or ideas before we analyse the film and the
procedures in detail?'

'I thought the initial communication between the
medical team arriving on the scene and the county
services was inadequate,' said someone from the
back, and Rachel sighed as she recognised the voice
of one of the union safety representatives renowned
for his attention to detail and resigned herself to a
lengthy session.

Five minutes later, however, the meeting was
interrupted by Michelle, the medical secretary, who
whispered something to Ron Banks.

Ron frowned then glanced up, his gaze coming to
rest on Rachel. 'Rachel, it appears the new medical
officer has arrived to look over the place. Personnel
have him in Reception at the moment. Should
Michelle tell them to bring him over?'

Rachel stood up. 'Yes, I'd better go and meet
him, Ron, if you'll excuse me. We must get off on
the right foot.'

'Let's hope he's a bit more receptive to accident
prevention than the last one,' said Ron cryptically as

Rachel made her way to the back of the room amid a murmur of amused assent.

It had been a well-known fact that their last medical officer had spent little time studying new methods of health and safety and accident prevention and there had been an ever-present air of friction between himself and Ron Banks. He had left suddenly while Rachel had been on leave and on her return she'd been told that another officer had been appointed but she'd had no time to find out anything about him. In fact, she thought, as she made her way through a section of the shop-floor and let herself into the occupational health centre, she didn't even know his name.

Rachel had been at OBEX for two years and was now senior sister in charge of the busy factory medical centre. She had decided on making her career in industrial nursing after leaving general nursing, even though at first she had had reservations and wondered if she had made the right move. But within six months she'd known she had been right, and she had now reached the stage where she thoroughly enjoyed her work.

Her colleague, Sister Nina Clarey, was on duty in the centre, and she looked round in surprise from the store cupboard where she was checking supplies and peered at Rachel over her glasses. 'I didn't expect you back yet,' she said. 'Those sessions usually go on for hours.'

'That one probably will,' said Rachel with a laugh, then, seeing Nina's expression, she explained, 'I had a message to say our new MO's arrived; I thought I should be here.'

Nina's eyes widened. 'I didn't think he was coming until tomorrow—gosh, I'm glad you came back.' She glanced anxiously round the treatment area.

'We're all tidy in here, aren't we? No problems?' asked Rachel, glancing quickly into the four-bedded rest-room, the offices and the staffroom, which all opened off the main reception and treatment area of the centre.

Nina had no time to answer as the main doors opened and Julie Weatherstone, one of the personnel officers, came into the centre accompanied by a tall man.

'Ah, Rachel, you're here. Good,' said Julie. 'I've brought your new MO to meet you.'

Rachel had a fleeting impression of mid-brown hair, clear grey eyes, clean-shaven strong features and a firm square jaw, then, not giving her time to even think, her hand was clasped in a firm handshake as Julie went on, 'Rachel, David Markham. Dr Markham, this is Sister Rachel Stevens.'

They stared at each other and Rachel wasn't sure who was the more surprised.

David Markham? It couldn't be *that* David Markham.

But it was. She hadn't set eyes on him for years, but there was no mistake.

He must have been equally surprised to see her but he recovered first, and while Rachel was still floundering to find something to say and Julie was murmuring something about hoping he would enjoy working at OBEX he said, 'Actually, we've met before. How are you, Rachel?'

She took a deep breath. 'Well, thank you, David. And you?'

He nodded and there followed an awkward silence where Julie and Nina must have become aware of the tension, for they glanced at each other at the same moment as a patient arrived in the centre.

Rachel asked the patient to sit in the small waiting area then turned as if to go and prepare herself to see to him.

'It's all right, Rachel,' said Nina quickly. 'I'll see to the patient.'

'No, Nina,' Rachel heard herself say, 'I would prefer it if you would show Dr Markham around, please.'

She was vaguely aware of Nina's look of surprise, and David Markham's raised eyebrows.

'Well, Doctor,' said Julie, 'I'll leave you to the tender mercies of these ladies.' She then beat a hasty retreat.

While Nina took David Markham into the office, Rachel called the patient through to the treatment area and pulled a screen round him. It was while she was looking for his record folder in the filing cabinet that she realised her hands were trembling.

The patient's name was Wayne Benfield and he'd been coming into the centre for daily dressings to an injured ankle. His ankle bone had been badly grazed a week before by a metal panel that he had been working on which had slipped from his grasp.

'How has it been, Wayne?' asked Rachel, making herself concentrate as she removed the old dressings.

'Much better the last couple of days.' He winced slightly as she gently probed the area for any sign of infection.

'Well, it's healed beautifully.' Rachel straightened up. 'I don't think we'll need to put another dressing on that.'

'You mean I don't need to come back any more?'

She shook her head. 'No, not unless you have more trouble, of course, but I don't think you will.'

He grinned and began pulling on his sock. 'Pity, I'd got used to my daily visits here to see you lovely ladies. You've no idea how it brightened up my day.'

He was still grinning when he left the centre and as Rachel began clearing up the soiled dressings she strained her ears to hear what was being said in the office. All she could hear, however, was a low murmur. She still hadn't got over the shock of seeing David Markham again; it must be. . .she did a rapid calculation in her head. . .all of five years since he'd walked out of their lives. She'd heard since that he'd left the health service and gone abroad to work. . . and now not only was he back, but she was expected to work with him.

She had no further time to think, however, as first one then two more patients arrived to be seen. One had a recurrence of an old back injury involving a disc which bulged from between the vertebrae from time to time, causing intense pain, and the other was a young secretary with period pains. Rachel gave the girl some analgesics for her pain, persuaded her to lie down on one of the beds then pulled the curtains around her to enable her to rest.

The back injury proved more complicated, however, and ended up with Rachel ringing the casualty unit at the local hospital who sent an ambulance for the patient. After checking that the proper procedures had been followed and that the incident had been fully recorded, Rachel contacted Louise Raymond, the factory welfare officer, and asked her to telephone the man's wife and inform her that he was being admitted to hospital.

By the time Rachel got back to her office, Nina was alone. Cautiously she looked round, expecting David Markham suddenly to appear.

'It's all right,' said Nina curiously, 'you can come in now, he's gone.'

Rachel sighed. 'Thank goodness for that. But no doubt he'll be back.'

'I would imagine so, seeing that he's going to be working here! What's wrong, Rachel?'

'Wrong?' Rachel paused by her desk and began toying with the telephone cord.

'Yes, it's pretty obvious you know him and that there's something wrong. It just isn't like you to leave me to it like that, especially with a new member of staff, and a medical officer at that.'

'I'm sorry, Nina, really I am.' Rachel sighed again. 'You're quite right, of course, I do know him.'

Nina stared at her, waiting for her to continue, and when she remained silent, without any warning she suddenly asked, 'Rachel, were you in love with him? Is that it?'

'In love. . .!' She looked up, shocked that Nina should even think such a thing.

'That's what I said; I just got the impression it might be something like that.' Nina frowned. 'Is it so improbable? After all, he's very handsome. . . don't you agree?'

'What? Oh, yes, I suppose he is handsome if you like that sort of thing, but. . .'

'But you weren't in love with him?'

'No, Nina, I wasn't in love with David Markham,' said Rachel firmly, then, seeing that Nina was still slightly bemused, she added, 'In fact, I think you could go so far as to say I detested him.'

Ten minutes later, after Nina had made mugs of tea for them both, the two women sat down in Rachel's office.

'Do you want to tell me about it?' Nina eyed her speculatively across the desk.

'There's not a great deal to tell.' Rachel leaned back in her chair. 'David Markham was once engaged to my sister Jennifer, that's all.'

'Your sister?' Nina's eyes narrowed. 'Didn't you once say she had multiple sclerosis?'

Rachel nodded, then took a sip of her tea. 'That's right. She was diagnosed five years ago, about the time David Markham went out of her life.'

Nina frowned. 'Are you saying he couldn't take it, that he broke off the engagement?'

'You can say what you like,' Rachel shrugged. 'All I know is he broke Jennifer's heart and his name has been taboo in our family ever since.'

'And now he's come to work with us. . .' said Nina slowly. 'You're going to find this very difficult, aren't you, Rachel?'

'Yes, I think I probably am. It certainly doesn't make for an ideal working relationship, does it?'

Nina fell silent for a moment then suddenly, looking up, she said, 'What happened to your sister? Where is she now?'

'She lives with my parents; they care for her round the clock. It's a full-time job; in fact I've just spent my leave there simply to give them a break for a few days.'

Nina stared at her then slowly she set her mug down on the desk. 'I had no idea,' she said quietly. 'Oh, I knew you had a sister who was disabled, but. . .' She trailed off helplessly. 'I don't know. . . you work with someone, you think you know them, but how little any of us really understand another's problems. . .'

'It's all right, Nina, really. I think we've all gradually come to terms with Jennifer's condition and learnt to make the best of it. . .but. . .' she stared at her telephone as it suddenly rang, her thoughts obviously far away '. . .but I don't think I'll ever forgive David Markham for the way he treated her,' she said at last as she stretched out her hand to answer the phone.

Rachel groaned as her alarm sounded the following Monday morning and, rolling over, she flicked the button to silence it, then lay for a few minutes staring at the ceiling. Then she remembered: today David Markham would be taking up his new position as medical officer at OBEX. Ever since she had realised that he was the new officer she had been dreading the moment they would have to actually start working together.

At the weekend she had visited her parents' home and spent some time with her sister, Jennifer, but she had found that she had been unable to tell them about David Markham. His name hadn't been mentioned in the Stevens household for a very long time and Rachel assumed that they all thought he was still abroad. She knew she would probably have to say something sooner or later, but she decided she would put it off as long as she possibly could. She knew Jennifer would be hurt at the mention of him and the poor girl had enough problems as it was without adding to them.

Getting out of bed, Rachel flung open the curtains and looked out at the September morning. The view from her top-floor flat never failed to please her as the whole city of Branchester stretched out before her: the cathedral with its spire gleaming in the early-morning sunlight, the buildings where ancient and modern blended together harmoniously, the

canal like a silver ribbon with its brightly painted
barges and the Norman boundary wall that enclosed
it all. The foliage in the park was turning to bur-
nished gold and Rachel knew that in a few short
weeks the temperature would drop, the leaves would
fall and once again her favourite time of year would
be over.

She showered and shampooed her short dark hair,
combing it into its neat bob, then she made toast
and coffee and sat for a few minutes before her
kitchen window which enjoyed the same view as her
bedroom. She'd been lucky to get this flat and at a
reasonable price, for accommodation in Branchester
wasn't easy to find. At one point it had looked as if
she might have been forced to live at home with her
parents, and much as Rachel loved them she knew
that arrangement just wouldn't work. Life was
fraught enough for the Stevenses as it was, with the
constant care of Jennifer, without her adding to their
problems, and besides, she had come to value her
privacy and her independence.

She'd become lost in her thoughts; with a sigh and
a reluctant glance at the kitchen clock she stood up,
drained her coffee-cup then went back to her bedroom to get dressed.

Fifteen minutes later she was behind the wheel of
her car on the out-of-city route. The Yorkshire
branch of OBEX Aircraft Corporation was five miles
north of Branchester, occupying an immense site
and employing a workforce of nearly five thousand.
It specialised in producing the fusillage for A272

Coachliners, which were then transported to another of the corporation's branches for assembling, and smaller ten-seater aircraft which were built, assembled and tested on the site.

It was just after seven-thirty when Rachel arrived at the factory's main entrance. It was fairly quiet as by that time the workforce had arrived and started their day shift and most of the night shift had already left.

The security guard on the gate was new and didn't recognise Rachel so she had to produce her pass. Her handbag had fallen behind the car seat when she'd stopped at the traffic lights in town so several minutes were lost as she scrabbled for her pass, then when she drove into the car park she couldn't immediately find a space and had to drive round several times. By the time she entered the building and hurried across to Occupational Health she was several minutes later than she liked to be in the mornings.

To her dismay, as she pushed open the door of the treatment-room the first person she set eyes on was David Markham.

'Oh, you're here already,' she said.

He was leaning against a table and he straightened up as she came in. 'I understood the shift started at seven-thirty,' he said.

'Well, yes, it does.' She slipped off her mac, trying not to appear flustered. 'But Dr Rowell never got here much before eight.'

'Didn't he?' David Markham raised his eyebrows,

giving Rachel the distinct impression that what his predecessor had done held no interest for him.

She didn't answer and he followed her into her office.

'We didn't have chance to talk the other day, as you were so busy,' he said, pushing the door to behind him.

Rachel swung round to face him. What did he mean—talk? Did he think she was going to discuss Jennifer and the past with him?

'Listen, Dr Markham, I don't think we need. . .'

'We need to discuss the hours I shall be here,' he intervened smoothly, and there was a hint of amusement in his cool grey eyes.

'What?' She stared at him, then suddenly felt foolish as she realised how uptight she'd allowed herself to become. 'Oh, yes, yes, of course,' she mumbled, turning away from him and walking behind her desk.

'I shall be here four mornings each week and two afternoons,' he said easily.

'Oh?' She looked up quickly, doing nothing to disguise her surprise at the fact that he would only apparently be at OBEX on a part-time basis.

He chose, however, to ignore her tone. 'I understand from your colleague that the bulk of my workload will be employment and management medicals with a smattering of daily casualties and a fair degree of stress counselling.'

'We certainly do a good deal of counselling these days,' Rachel agreed. 'It will be up to you how much you participate, just as it will be up to you how far you are prepared to go in our health and safety campaigns.'

'I understand my predecessor wasn't too interested in that line of business.'

'No, Dr Markham, unfortunately he wasn't. Graham Rowell was only concerned with how he was going to treat a condition or an injury; he said it wasn't his job to worry about how it could have been prevented in the first place.'

'In actual fact, he was quite right.'

Rachel swung round indignantly from the filing cabinet which she had just unlocked ready to take out the records for that morning's surgery.

'It's OK.' He held up his hands. 'As it happens, I think prevention is better than cure, but in some cases I've found that safety procedures leave a lot to be desired.'

'I'm sure you won't find that's the case here at OBEX,' said Rachel crisply. 'In fact our regulations have been the envy of other companies, and we're constantly striving to find ways of improving things.'

'I'm sure your methods are very efficient, Sister.'

She looked up sharply; his tone had been faintly mocking and the amusement was still in his eyes. It was almost as if he was using their past acquaintance as an excuse for familiarity. She felt a sudden surge of anger. If he thought he could do that he needed to be put right. She took a deep breath but before she had the chance to speak someone tapped on the door and a dark, bearded man appeared.

He glanced quickly from one to the other as if aware of the tension then said, 'Would you like me to come back later?'

'No, of course not, Alan.' Rachel pulled herself together. 'Come in. This is David Markham, our new medical officer. Dr Markham, this is Charge Nurse Alan Hill; he's just finished the night shift.'

After the two men had shaken hands she thankfully escaped, leaving them to talk while she went out to prepare the treatment-room for the first of the morning's patients.

They worked steadily, dealing first with patients who had come for audio testing, an important part of the health screening programmes that were regularly carried out on members of the workforce. The level of noise on the shop-floor was very high and the quality of hearing had to be carefully assessed and monitored and, if necessary, steps taken to prevent further deterioration.

Both Rachel and Nina got on well with the men, who in turn liked and respected the nursing team, and usually there was an easy-going air of camaraderie in the centre.

That morning, however, Rachel was only aware of the presence of the new medical officer and the atmosphere was tense and strained. It must have transmitted itself to the patients, for even they gave up after their initial attempts at jollity, and by mid-morning a definite air of gloom seemed to have settled over the place. Even the factory ambulance driver, Greg Bradshaw, who was renowned for being able to cheer the most dire of situations, seemed subdued.

'This is a right palace of fun this morning, isn't it?' he said as he came into their tiny staff-room for coffee. 'What's up with everyone?'

There was an embarrassed silence and Nina glanced at Rachel, then at David Markham, then with a murmured apology she hurried from the room.

Greg looked round in amazement. 'Was it something I said?' Even his usual gap-toothed grin was absent now.

Rachel shook her head. 'No, Greg,' she said, 'it isn't you.' As the driver ambled off, shaking his head, she stood up, took a deep breath, then shut the door of the staff-room before turning to the new medical officer.

'I think, Dr Markham,' she said firmly, 'if we are to improve the atmosphere around here and have a reasonable working relationship, there are one or two things that need to be said to clear the air.'

# CHAPTER TWO

'I WAS thinking the same thing,' David said calmly. 'What is it you want to discuss?'

Rachel stared at him. Surely he couldn't be ignorant of the reason for her coolness towards him?

Not waiting for her to answer, he went on. 'It was pretty obvious that you weren't too happy when you knew I was going to be working here. I admit when I saw you I was pretty surprised myself and I accept that my previous involvement with your sister could be a source of embarrassment——'

'I think——'

'However,' he continued smoothly, not giving Rachel a chance to say anything, 'if we are to create a harmonious atmosphere, not only for ourselves but for everyone else on this unit, then I think we have to agree not to discuss the past. What do you say?'

'Well, yes.' She hesitated, then went on, 'Yes, Dr Markham, I would go so far as to say that forgetting the past is the only way we're going to achieve any sort of working relationship.'

She frowned; she might be prepared to forget the past to help the work situation, but she had no intention of letting this man think she had forgiven what he had done in the past. She opened her mouth to try to put this fact into words, but he intervened again.

'One thing we do need to stop is all this Doctor, Sister business. I think we know each other well enough to use our Christian names.'

Almost against her will she found herself nodding.

'Right, that's settled, then.' He walked to the door, then paused with one hand on the handle and looked back at her. 'There is just one thing I want to ask, then I won't refer to the past again.' When Rachel remained silent, he said, 'How is Jennifer?'

Rachel looked up sharply but his expression was inscrutable, giving away nothing of what he might be feeling. She took a deep breath. 'She's as well as can be expected in the circumstances. The disease progressed rapidly and there's been little or no remission.'

'Does she live with your parents?'

'She has to,' replied Rachel, returning his gaze. 'She needs constant attention.'

'Of course,' he murmured, glancing down at the desk.

And that, thought Rachel as she watched him carefully, was something you just weren't prepared to give. You couldn't face the thought of a handicapped wife so you hightailed it off the scene and out of her life. She longed to say it to his face, but somehow she couldn't quite bring herself to do so, especially as they had just agreed to try to bring about a better working relationship.

'Are we decided, then, Rachel?' He glanced at

her almost as if he was reading her thoughts. 'That we try to achieve a friendlier environment?' He smiled, and there was a glint in his eyes that made Rachel catch her breath. Surely he couldn't be trying to chat her up?

'Certainly,' she replied firmly. Then, putting paid to any ideas he might have, she added, 'On condition that that is how it remains: a friendly environment purely for working purposes.'

He stared at her, then inclined his head slightly in response. 'If that's how you want it. . .'

'Yes, David,' she said crisply, 'that's how I want it.'

The telephone rang at that moment; Rachel answered it and before David had time to leave the room she said, 'There's been an accident in the canteen—a boiler has blown up and two of the staff have been scalded.'

'Then what are we waiting for?' He stepped aside, allowing her to precede him.

Greg drove them in the factory ambulance across the busy shop-floor, through one of the main entrances and across the grounds to the building that housed the canteen. On arrival in the kitchens they found that the domestic superintendent had followed the correct first-aid procedure for scalds and burns and the two ladies, although suffering from shock, had already had ice packs administered to their injuries.

'Well done,' said David to the superintendent

after he'd examined the scalds. 'Your quick thinking has probably prevented even any blistering.'

'We'll take you two back to the centre to rest and recover,' said Rachel, then, looking up at the superintendent who was hovering anxiously, she asked, 'Has the incident been recorded in the accident book?'

The woman nodded. 'Yes, Sister.'

'And do we have witnesses to what exactly happened?'

'Yes, I'll get a written report from them and let Management have it. I've also reported the incident to Maintenance.'

'I trust there'll be an enquiry as to whether or not the boiler was faulty?' asked David, as he assisted one of the two casualties to her feet.

'Of course.' The superintendent was looking relieved that the incident had not been as bad as it might have been.

When they returned to the centre Rachel and Nina applied light dressings to the scalds, then took the two ladies into the rest-room and gave them sweet tea to help them recover from shock. By that time there were several other patients to be seen, including two for employment medicals. One of these, a young man called Steve Fields, had applied for a job as a paint sprayer. His medical went well until he revealed that he suffered from asthma and David pointed out to him that he would never cope with that particular job. He was then given an application form for a job in another department where hopefully his asthma wouldn't be aggravated.

By the end of the day the atmosphere had definitely improved in the centre, but whenever Rachel found herself working directly with David Markham she was aware of tension between the two of them. His working methods were very different from those of Graham Rowell and she found she was constantly on her toes to try and keep one step ahead of him in anticipating what he would want next.

For once she was relieved when her shift was over and it was time to go home. The whole day had been a great strain and although they had attempted to resolve their differences and clear the air Rachel found herself dreading the prospect of working with David Markham on a permanent basis.

The situation didn't improve much during the rest of the week and for the first time since Rachel had been working at OBEX she found herself not looking forward to going to work in the mornings.

Then at the weekend she paid her usual visit to her family. Rachel's father, Ken Stevens, had been in insurance all his life, and the family lived in a comfortable detached home on the outskirts of the city. Her mother, Valerie, had returned to teaching after her family were off her hands, but she had been forced to give up her job to give Jennifer the care she needed.

They all had a meal together, then, as the September evening was warm, Ken Stevens wheeled

Jennifer's wheelchair outside and Valerie carried a tray of coffee on to the patio.

Rachel found herself watching her sister closely as they all sat and talked. Jennifer was thirty now, as fair as Rachel was dark, taking after their father, while Rachel favoured Valerie for colouring. Her sister's illness had taken its toll on her looks and they had all spent some very traumatic moments helping her to come to terms with the debilitating condition which had now rendered her legs virtually useless.

Rachel had already decided not to mention anything about the new MO at OBEX. There was no reason for Jennifer to know and it would probably only upset her, but Rachel did find herself wondering about Jennifer's previous relationship with David Markham.

At the time Rachel herself had still been doing her training but they had all worked at the same hospital — David as a senior house officer and Jennifer as a staff nurse on Orthopaedics. Rachel hadn't taken a lot of notice of the young SHO — she had been more interested in her own circle of friends at the time — but he had been a frequent visitor at the Stevenses' home and she knew her parents had liked him and had been pleased at the prospect of him becoming their son-in-law.

Rachel had become so lost in her thoughts that she suddenly realised her father had been talking to her and she hadn't heard a word.

'Sorry, Dad.' She looked up sharply, almost spilling her coffee. 'What were you saying?'

'You were miles away.' He smiled, leaned forward and as he set his cup and saucer down on the pink paving stones of the patio Rachel thought how grey his hair had turned. 'I was simply asking how work was going.'

'Oh, not so bad; it's been a busy week, lots of medicals and a casualty-faking exercise.'

'What was it this time?' Jennifer looked up with sudden interest and Rachel knew she liked to hear about her work. 'Another air crash?'

Rachel shook her head. 'No, not this time; it was a bomb that supposedly went off without any warning—lots of gory casualties.'

'Did you say a bomb? At OBEX?' Valerie Stevens had been in the house to get more coffee and as she stepped through the patio doors she stood for a moment staring at Rachel in horror, having only heard the last part of the conversation. Jennifer's illness had had its effect on her too; lately her nerves had been bad and she hadn't been sleeping.

'No, it's all right, Mum,' Rachel hastened to reassure her. 'It was a casualty-faking—you know, making sure we would know what to do in such a situation.'

'God forbid.' Valerie shuddered and set the coffee-pot down on the white wrought-iron table.

'Did you get your new medical officer?' asked Ken Stevens suddenly, and Rachel stiffened. 'You did say old Rowell had gone, didn't you?'

'Er — yes, Dad, I did, and yes, the new man has started.'

'And?'

'Sorry?' She glanced up, trying to appear nonchalant.

'What's he like? This new chap?'

'Oh, he's OK; his ideas certainly seem to be more in tune with OBEX policies than Graham Rowell's ever were.'

Her father nodded his approval and for one moment Rachel thought he was going to ask the new MO's name.

The moment passed, her mother began talking about the late roses in her flowerbeds and Rachel was just thinking she'd got away with not mentioning David Markham, when her father said, 'Talking of OBEX, we wanted to check the date of the Family Day with you.' He glanced at his wife as he spoke.

Rachel sat up straight. She'd forgotten all about Family Day. 'Oh. . .it isn't until next month. . . I'll have to check the exact date,' she mumbled, then, glancing round at the others, she said, 'Are you quite sure you want to go again? I expect it will be much the same as last year.'

'Of course we do,' her father replied. 'We're looking forward to it and it'll make a nice day out for Jennifer.'

Rachel gave a weak smile and lifted up her cup for more coffee.

It wasn't until later when she was helping her mother to wash up and her father was still outside with Jennifer that Rachel had the opportunity to explain the situation.

'David Markham?' Her mother's eyes widened. 'Don't say he's back on the scene again. I thought we'd seen the last of him, after what he did to Jennifer.'

'So did I,' said Rachel. 'But he's back and he's working at OBEX and there's nothing I can do about it. I wasn't even going to mention it today, but I'd forgotten about Family Day until Dad brought it up just now.'

'Do you think he'll be there?'

Rachel shrugged. 'I should think there's a very good chance. The only consolation is that there'll be a few thousand others there as well. We'll just have to try and make sure they don't meet.'

'I wouldn't want Jennifer upset again.' Her mother began wiping her hands. 'She's been through enough.'

'Does she mention David these days?' asked Rachel curiously, looking out of the window at Jennifer sitting on the patio in her wheelchair talking to her father.

'No.' Her mother shook her head. 'When they broke up it was as if she never wanted to hear his name again—and I can't say I blame her. He couldn't really have loved her, Rachel, if he couldn't face what happened to her—and him a doctor as well!'

'It was probably because he was a doctor that he couldn't face the future—he knew what to expect,' said Rachel bitterly, then as she caught sight of her mother's expression she said hurriedly, 'Oh, I'm not making excuses for him, I'm just stating a fact.'

'Has he changed?' asked her mother after a moment.

Rachel shook her head. 'No, he looks exactly the same. It was a shock, I can tell you, when he walked into the centre and I realised he was my new medical officer.'

'I wouldn't imagine he'd bargained on finding you there either.'

'That's true.' She gave a short laugh. 'I'm not sure who was the more surprised.'

'I thought he'd gone abroad.'

'He had. Apparently he's been working in Australia, on oil rigs, I believe.'

'Pity he hadn't stayed there.' There was bitterness in her mother's voice now. 'I shouldn't say anything to your father if I were you, not tonight anyway.'

'What will his reaction be?'

'I would think just the sound of David Markham's name would set him off.'

'Oh, dear! That bad?'

'Yes, you'd better let me tell him later.'

'How's Jennifer been this week?'

Valerie Stevens sighed. 'Not too good. Her vision's been very blurred and she's had another urinary tract infection.'

'I thought she seemed depressed.'

'Yes, she has been. That's why we were looking

forward to the Family Day. It's the one thing she's seemed to want to go to.'

'Don't worry about it, Mum. I'm sure everything will be all right.'

By the time Rachel left the house to drive back into town she was feeling really savage towards David Markham, then she had to remind herself that, in spite of the fact that they all felt bitterness at the way he had walked out on Jennifer, it wasn't his fault that her sister had multiple sclerosis.

It had been a dreadful day for the Stevens family when Jennifer's diagnosis had been confirmed, a day that Rachel would never forget. Her mother had telephoned her at the nurses' home where she had been living and had asked her if she could come home. She had guessed that the reason was something to do with Jennifer for she had known that her sister hadn't been well for some while and had been undergoing tests since experiencing stabbing pain in her right eye and numbness in her legs.

They had always been a close family and that night they had all ended up in tears after a lengthy talk with their family GP who had come to the house to talk to them about Jennifer's diagnosis.

In her case the disease had progressed rapidly with little instances of remission and her condition had deteriorated so much that within three years she was almost permanently confined to a wheelchair.

As Rachel reached her flat and let herself in she found herself trying to remember whether David had been there that evening when her mother had sent for her. It was hard to be certain but she was pretty sure he hadn't, and she imagined she must have assumed he was on duty at the hospital. Whichever way, she probably hadn't given it much thought at the time and it had been some time later when her mother had told her that he had left the country and gone abroad to work.

At that point Jennifer had just had to give up her own job as she had found it impossible to continue nursing and Rachel could clearly remember the night she'd found her sister severely depressed about her future. Jennifer had sobbed in her arms as all her dreams — of her nursing career, and of becoming a wife and mother — had flown. She hadn't mentioned David Markham but his presence had hung between them like a spectre and his name hadn't been mentioned since. It had all been a far cry from the excitement of her engagement to the handsome young houseman when the Stevenses had celebrated with a party in the garden of their home. To Rachel that all now seemed as if it had been in another time, another world and it had only been in the last few days with the reappearance of David Markham that the memories had been revived.

But one thing Rachel was certain of was that the revival of those memories had only intensified her dislike of her sister's ex-fiancé, and when she arrived for work the following Monday morning and he was the first person she saw she found her resolve to have as little to do with him as possible had only been strengthened.

'Good weekend?' he asked as she hung up her jacket in the narrow passageway outside her office.

'Yes, thank you,' she replied shortly, intending to slip past him to the treatment area to begin preparing for the first of the morning's patients.

He, however, seemed to have other ideas and stood in her way.

'So what did you do?'

'I beg your pardon?' She stared frostily at him.

'At the weekend, what did you do?'

'I can't see that could possibly interest you.'

'How can you be so sure?' Again the maddening glimmer of amusement was in his eyes.

'Oh, for goodness' sake, David, we have work to do.' Again she attempted to push past him. But still he made no attempt to move.

'David!'

He smiled then at her exasperation. 'Yes, I suppose we had better get on, although I'd much rather stay here and hear what you've been doing, and I would be interested, in spite of what you might think.' He moved aside but not right out of the narrow passageway and she was forced to squeeze past him. The rough tweed of his jacket brushed her cheek and she caught the scent of soap and his aftershave.

To her dismay she felt her cheeks grow hot, and by the time she reached the treatment area she found the first of her patients had arrived. In a desperate attempt to concentrate, and ignore David who had followed her, she turned her attention to the burly shop-floor worker who awaited her.

Jack Rogers was a man of fifty who had worked on the shop-floor all his working life. He had come into the centre that morning complaining of indigestion.

'It's probably only the wife's roast yesterday, Sister,' he said to Rachel almost sheepishly. 'Maybe you could give me a dose of bicarb — that'll shift it.'

'Have you had this before, Jack?' Rachel asked as she found his records and began flicking through his folder.

'Once or twice,' he admitted, 'but bicarb generally puts it right.'

'Where exactly is the pain?'

'All over really.' He indicated his chest.

'Have you seen your own GP about it?'

He shook his head. 'No, you can't go to the doctor every time you get a bit of wind. I only came over here because the super said I had to.'

'Quite right too,' said Rachel. 'Now, Jack, if you'll just slip your arm out of your overalls — that's right — I want to check your blood-pressure.'

A few moments later as Rachel released the cuff from Jack Rogers' arm after noting a reading of a hundred and seventy over ninety, she said, 'I'm going to ask our doctor to have a look at you, Jack.'

'New bloke you've got here, isn't it?' he asked, then when she nodded he suddenly looked alarmed and said, 'Nothing wrong, is there, Sister?'

'I shouldn't think so, Jack,' she replied briskly,

'but I'd like the doctor to check you over and maybe do a few tests.'

'Tests? What sort of tests?'

'Nothing to worry yourself about, Jack. Just sit there quietly for a few minutes and I'll see if the doctor is free.'

She found David in his room talking to one of the superintendents. He looked up as she came in and to her irritation she saw the amusement was back in his eyes.

'Ah, Rachel,' he said without giving her a chance to say what she had come for. 'Martin here ——' he indicated the man at his side ' — is having a problem with one of his staff. He suspects alcohol abuse and wants to know if we would consider counselling.'

'Of course,' Rachel replied. 'When would you like us to start?' She turned to the superintendent.

'The man's problems have intensified in the last few weeks and it's reached the stage where he's late at least three mornings a week now.'

'Is it anyone I know?' she asked, wishing that David would stop staring at her.

'His name's Len Seager.'

She frowned, shaking her head, then as the name rang a bell in her mind she looked up quickly. 'Oh, yes, I do know Len. I remember him from his hearing tests — a quiet man. Do you think you could get him to come in and talk to us?'

'That could be the difficult part; you see, he doesn't think he has a problem.'

'In that case it would be better if you brought us up to date with what's been happening first.'

'Do you mean now?' The superintendent looked at David.

'I'm not sure this is a convenient time. . .' David turned to Rachel and raised his eyebrows. 'You were looking for me, Sister?'

'Yes, Dr Markham, I was,' she nodded then looked back at the other man. 'Could you come back after lunch?'

He hesitated. 'Yes, that should be all right. About two o'clock?' When Rachel nodded in response, he went on, 'Thank you both. I want to get this problem sorted out—Len's a good man and I don't want to lose him.'

The superintendent went back to the shop-floor and David looked at Rachel. 'You're happy to deal with this on your own?'

She frowned. 'What do you mean?'

'Asking the superintendent to come back after lunch?'

'I thought you might be prepared to be there as well. . .but if you don't consider this is in your line of business. . .don't worry, I'm quite used to it; Graham Rowell couldn't be bothered with counselling either, but I happen to think. . .'

'Calm down,' he said maddeningly. 'That wasn't what I meant at all.'

'Then what. . .?' she frowned.

'I'm not here this afternoon. Maybe you'd forgotten?'

She stared at him, then to her annoyance she once more felt the colour touch her cheeks. 'Yes, I had forgotten,' she muttered at last. 'I'm not used to people who only work part-time. But while you are here, if it isn't too much trouble, perhaps you'd take a look at a patient.' The sarcasm in her tone was not lost on David and he grimaced as he followed her out of the office.

# CHAPTER THREE

DAVID examined Jack Rogers and, suspecting an angina attack, asked Rachel to perform an electrocardiogram. The results confirmed his diagnosis and after he had written a report for Jack's own GP transport was arranged to take the patient home to rest.

Later, while Rachel was checking supplies, Nina happened to mention that the new MO seemed to be proving more popular with the staff than the previous one had been, then added, 'Just as long as they don't think he's a soft touch and that they can come in here with a finger ache and think he'll send them home.' She grinned at Rachel.

'If they're thinking that, they should be put straight,' said Rachel grimly. 'David Markham's no soft touch, believe me. I can assure you he's a very hard man.'

'I wouldn't think you were too afraid of him,' observed Nina.

'I'm not,' Rachel replied shortly. 'I'm simply saying we shouldn't underestimate him.'

After lunch, Martin Foulds, the superintendent, came back to speak to Rachel about Len Seager.

'How much exactly do you need to know, Sister?' he asked as he came into her office and sat down.

'As much as you can remember.' Rachel sat back in her chair, preparing herself to listen.

'I would imagine alcohol started to become a problem for Len when his wife left him about three years ago,' Martin began. 'The standard of his work deteriorated and that was when we first suspected he might have a problem. On one occasion when he was late for work I questioned him and he said he had missed the bus. I was surprised as I knew Len usually drove his own car to work. Anyway,' he went on, 'I made some further enquiries and it transpired that Len had been convicted on a drink-driving offence and had lost his driving licence. Since then, he has been late on numerous occasions and we believe his alcohol consumption has increased. Some mornings he's suffering from what quite obviously is a hangover and at other times he appears to have a stomach upset. It's rapidly reaching the stage where he's becoming a danger, not only to himself, but to others on the shop-floor.'

'And he still refuses to accept he has a problem?' Rachel asked. Martin nodded. 'Well, that's the first thing we have to make him see, then we need to get him to come in for regular counselling sessions.'

'It won't be easy.' Martin Foulds shook his head.

'Supposing the next time he appears to be suffering from a stomach upset, or a hangover, for that matter,' said Rachel thoughtfully, 'you were to persuade him to come in here simply for some medication?'

'Well, we could try.'

'It would be a start, and we could take it from there. We would tread very carefully but we have done this sort of thing before and we would try and make him realise just what he's doing to himself.'

'Very well, Sister, thank you.' The superintendent stood up. 'Will Dr Markham be involved?'

'Of course.'

'I was rather hoping he was going to be here this afternoon.'

'He's off duty, I'm afraid.' Rachel found she had to almost bite her tongue to prevent herself making some comment.

Staff facilities at OBEX included a social club and leisure complex which were the envy of many other companies in the area. The complex included squash courts, an indoor swimming-pool and a gym, and Rachel, who had always loved swimming, took advantage of every opportunity she had to visit the complex. One evening after she'd completed a couple of laps of the pool she was surprised to see David Markham stroll out of the changing-rooms on to the poolside. As far as she knew, he had never before used the recreational facilities at OBEX.

He didn't appear to have seen her in the water and Rachel had the advantage of watching him unobserved as he strolled along the poolside, a towel slung around his neck. His lean, muscular body was tanned, presumably from his years in Australia, and while the hair on his legs had turned to gold the triangle of hair on his chest was dark and tapered away to a point at the base of his flat stomach, disappearing beneath the band of his black swimming-trunks.

It wasn't difficult for Rachel to understand what her sister had seen in this man, and just for a moment she found herself reluctantly acknowledging the fact that if she didn't know what she did about him she too would find him very attractive.

Almost as if he sensed her watching him, his eyes met hers across the pool. Their gaze locked for a long moment as he pulled the towel from his neck and flung it over a rail, then, suddenly embarrassed, she looked away. She heard rather than saw him dive into the water and a moment later he surfaced beside her.

'Do you come here often?' His grin was unexpected after the intensity of his stare and she found herself smiling back.

'Very often. I love swimming.'

He smoothed his hair back. 'So do I; it's one of the things I've been missing about Australia — that and the sun.'

'Well, we can't always guarantee the sun, but the pool's the next best thing to the sea.' Treading water, she moved to the side of the pool and, stretching out her arms, leaned back against the smooth tiles.

For a moment he was still, apparently watching her, then, just as she would have turned away from his apparent scrutiny, he said, 'Come on, I'll race you.' He struck out in a strong crawl stroke.

'That's not fair,' gasped Rachel, 'I've already done a couple of laps!' Nevertheless she followed him and for the next quarter of an hour they streaked up and down the pool.

In the end it was Rachel who was forced to give in and she swam to the side of the pool, climbed up the steps, and sat on the side watching as David completed several more laps.

At last he joined her, shaking the water from his hair and grabbing his towel from the rails where he had left it. By that time the pool was getting crowded as a shift ended and staff poured in for a swim before going home.

'It's good to see the pool being used so much,' he observed.

She nodded. 'Some people needed a lot of encouragement when it first opened, but now it's hard to find a time when it isn't crowded.' She looked up at him as she spoke and he held out his hand to help her to her feet. For one moment she hesitated, wary of touching him, but conscious that it would appear decidedly petty to ignore his gesture. At last she stretched out her own hand, but as he took it he allowed it to rest briefly in his before he tightened his grip, applying the necessary force to assist her to her feet.

But even then, when she was standing upright beside him, he made no attempt to release her hand and Rachel was only too aware of his appraising glance as he glanced down at the wet jade swimsuit tightly moulded to her slight, almost boyish figure before abruptly she snatched her hand away and walked quickly to the changing-rooms.

In the privacy of the cubicle she was aware that her heart was beating very fast. Angry with herself for reacting to him, she peeled off her wet swimsuit and vigorously began to towel her body. When she emerged some fifteen minutes later she found David dressed in sweatshirt and jeans, apparently waiting for her.

'I'm going to the club for a drink; care to join me?' he asked casually.

Her first reaction was to say no. Swimming was one thing, going for a drink was something else entirely, and would probably give him all sorts of ideas. But his request had been so casual that to refuse would have seemed as if she was making an issue. She nodded in what she hoped was an equally casual manner and followed him across the crowded foyer to the social club.

She asked for an orange juice, and while he was at the bar she found a table in the window. He joined her a few minutes later carrying her drink and a glass of lager for himself. He sat down opposite her and raised his glass.

'To auld acquaintance,' he said.

Before she had time to think, she'd raised her own glass in response and it was only after she'd sipped her drink that she realised what she'd done. Now he would have even more cause to think he could use their past acquaintance as an excuse to be familiar with her. But by then it was too late to withdraw, as

David had gulped several mouthfuls of his lager and had set his glass back on the table.

'So what have you been doing with yourself for the last five years?' he asked, leaning back in his chair and looking quizzically at her.

'I beg your pardon?' Startled by the suddenness of the question, she set her own glass down and stared back at him.

'I asked what you'd been doing for the last five years. . .'

'Yes, I know, but. . . I thought we'd agreed not to. . .'

'Not to discuss the past?' he asked. 'Yes, we did, but I understood that to mean my relationship with your sister. That ended five years ago. I was simply asking what you've been doing since.'

She gave a slight shrug. 'Oh, this and that,' she said evasively. She didn't really want to get into a conversation of that sort with David Markham and she certainly didn't want him knowing all about her personal life.

He, however, was not to be so easily put off.

'When I last saw you, you were barely out of your teens; in fact you were still doing your training if I remember rightly.' He raised one eyebrow when Rachel remained silent.

She nodded.

'So what happened after you'd qualified? Did you stay at St Clare's?'

'Yes, for a couple of years, then I moved to the General in Leeds where I was on Orthopaedics.'

'Why did you move into industry?'

'I wanted to be nearer home and there weren't any vacancies in the local hospitals at that particular time. I happened to see the post advertised with OBEX so I applied and got the job.'

'So are you living at home?' He frowned slightly and leaned forward.

She shook her head. 'No, I have a flat in town.'

He was silent for a moment, then he said, 'But you wanted to be nearer to your home?'

She took a deep breath, faintly irritated by his line of questioning. 'Yes, I wanted to be nearer home to be able to give my parents a hand with Jennifer. It's a full-time job looking after an MS patient,' she added, then glanced quickly at him to see what effect her words had.

He merely nodded, however, as if he as a doctor fully appreciated the difficulties and while Rachel was searching for what to say next he said, 'I couldn't believe it when I found you working here.'

'I noticed you looked pretty stunned,' she said drily.

'I didn't realise it was you at first.'

'Have I changed that much in five years?'

He put his head on one side and regarded her. 'Yes and no,' he said at last.

'What's that supposed to mean?'

'Well, you are still as slim as a reed—coltish, I believe your father used to say—you still have the same intriguing green eyes and those slanting eyebrows. . .'

'For goodness' sake. . .' She was half laughing now, finding it hard to be annoyed at what he was saying.

'And you still have that shiny dark hair, even though it's cut short now, but. . .'

'But what?' She sounded indignant now and a smile touched his lips.

'You've grown up. The girl has become a woman.'

She stared at him and, as her eyes met his, once again, like the moment he'd seen her in the pool, she seemed unable to look away. She was aware of the colour touching her cheeks and in confusion she tore her gaze from his, picked up her glass, took a mouthful of orange juice and stared with furious intent into the depths of her glass.

He remained silent, watching her, and her embarrassment grew until in the end she set her glass down with a bang and in desperation said, 'So are you going to tell me what's been happening to you in the last five years?'

She didn't really want to know. She couldn't care less what he had been up to, but quite suddenly it had become imperative that she steer the conversation away from herself and divert the interest he was showing in her.

'I've been in Australia for the entire time. I've been working for a company that constructs oil rigs and my job involved a lot of moving around.'

'Did you enjoy the work?'

'Very much.'

'And yet now you've come back?'

'Yes, now I've come back.'

He began toying with a beermat while Rachel, emboldened by his leading questions about her, went on, 'May one ask why, if you were enjoying it out there as much as you say you were?'

His hesitation was barely perceptible. 'It was for personal reasons.'

She glanced sharply at him, and although his expression remained inscrutable she had the fleeting impression that his reasons involved a woman. She felt a sudden surge of anger. He obviously made a habit of this. No doubt there was some poor woman in Australia with whom he'd become involved and from whom he'd run away when she'd presented him with some difficult situation.

Abruptly she drained her glass and stood up, aware of David's surprised expression as he looked up at her.

'I must be going,' she said tersely, then, picking up her bag, she added, 'Thanks for the drink.' As she walked from the club she was aware of his eyes on her.

Her anger and resentment grew as she drove home and for the rest of that evening she found it difficult to get David Markham out of her mind.

To her annoyance she found that just for a while there, while they had been swimming and afterwards when they'd first gone into the club, she had actually been enjoying his company. Then he had spoilt it by saying that his reasons for leaving Australia had been personal, and she had assumed he had been involved in a similar situation to that with Jennifer.

But maybe she'd jumped to conclusions, she thought uneasily as she prepared for bed; maybe it hadn't been anything like that at all. Maybe she had misjudged him.

Then she had to shake herself; what was she saying? Was she implying to herself that she didn't want anything to spoil the new friendly relationship that had arisen that evening?

Of course she wasn't. She didn't want to be friends with David Markham and that was that. She thought it outrageous that he should even think she might want to be friends in the circumstances. It was enough that she had to work with him.

And yet. . .the thought crept back just before she drifted off to sleep. . .it had been rather nice that he had actually noticed her in the past, and noticed her to such an extent that he was now in a position to compare the woman she'd become to the girl she'd once been.

When she awoke the next morning, however, she was able to put all such thoughts firmly from her mind as she simply strengthened her resolve to keep her relationship with David Markham purely on a professional basis.

When they met at work Rachel remained so cool with him that by the end of the week it was as if the little interlude in the pool and the club had never happened. They both became totally involved in their work, which included several management medicals and a series of talks on health and safety at work and accident prevention. These talks were presented both at management level and to shop-floor workers, and all the medical team became involved, mainly at David's instigation.

'He's certainly a different kettle of fish from old Rowell, isn't he?' said Greg Bradshaw one afternoon to Rachel and Nina.

'I know.' Nina smiled. 'Ron Banks can't believe his luck; David's even sent in requests for updated safety masks for the paint sprayers to use. Apparently he says the old ones were totally inadequate.'

'The thing is, Management will listen to him and he'll get what he wants, not like poor old Ron who's been waffling away for years and not getting anywhere. No——' Greg shook his head '—I think Dr Markham's the best thing to happen to this unit for a very long time—don't you, Rachel?'

When Rachel didn't immediately reply Nina peered over her glasses at Greg and said, 'I think you may find Rachel is the one person who may disagree with you.'

'Why?' Greg turned in surprise and looked at Rachel who was sitting at her desk writing up some reports.

She shrugged. 'Oh, it's a personal thing, Greg, nothing to do with his work.'

A slow grin spread over the ambulance driver's face. 'Oh, I see,' he said with a knowing smile at Nina.

'What do you see?' Rachel frowned, slightly irritated by his manner.

'You saying it's a personal thing between you and the doc — that explains things.'

'Explains what?' Rachel stared up at him in growing exasperation.

He grinned again. 'It's pretty obvious, isn't it? Why, even the blokes on the jig were saying only this morning. . .'

'Greg, I think you'd better go and get on with your work,' Nina intervened briskly, but by that time Rachel had risen to her feet, her face flaming.

Greg glanced uncertainly from Rachel to Nina but as he turned to the door Rachel stopped him.

'Just what were they saying, Greg?'

He looked uncomfortable then and shuffled his feet. 'Oh, nothing, Rachel, you know how it is,' he mumbled.

'No, Greg, I don't know how it is. You tell me. What is it people have been saying?'

He glanced at Nina for support but by this time she was staring at the ground. He took a deep breath. 'Only that the doc fancies you something rotten.' He said it in a rush, then with one last sheepish grin he disappeared, leaving Rachel staring at the door.

'Is that what people are saying?' Wildly she turned and looked at Nina, who gave an embarrassed laugh.

'Seriously, Nina, I want to know.'

'I'm sure there's no harm in it, Rachel. Don't get

yourself upset; you know how they all love to gossip. . .'

'But how did it start, for heaven's sake?' Rachel ran her fingers through her hair in a distracted fashion.

Nina hesitated, then, obviously realising that Rachel wasn't going to move until she had an answer, she said, 'Apparently someone saw you swimming with him. . .'

'For God's sake! We just happened to be in the pool at the same time, that's all.'

Nina didn't answer.

Rachel shot her a glance. 'Surely you don't think there was anything in that? Honestly, Nina, you know how I feel about David Markham. After the way he treated my sister, I wouldn't go with him if he were the last man on earth.'

Nina was silent for a moment then as she glanced up Rachel noticed a smile hovering about her lips. 'Not even for a drink in the social club?'

She stared at her then turned away in exasperation. 'I simply had a drink after we came out of the pool; surely you can't read anything into that?'

'Maybe I wouldn't.' Nina smiled. 'But that lot out there might.' She jerked her head in the direction of the factory shop-floor. 'Come on, Rachel, you've been here long enough to know how they love anything like this, especially when it involves one of us or one of the management team.'

'Well, they can just think again,' replied Rachel hotly, 'and if anyone says anything to you on those

lines I would be obliged if you would put them
straight.' Angrily she turned to the door and yanked
it open, almost colliding with David Markham who
was standing on the threshold.

For one moment her eyes met his and fleetingly
she wondered how much he had heard.

He frowned then. 'Is anything wrong?' he asked,
and when she shook her head he added, 'You seem
upset about something.'

Furiously she pushed past him, leaving Nina to
make any explanation she considered suitable.

Not only was she angry, she was dismayed by
what Nina had said, that rumours of that nature
should be circulating the factory linking her name
with David Markham's. This was the last thing she
had envisaged and she knew full well that if the
rumours had reached her ears there was a very good
chance he too would have heard them.

She stalked out of the factory, intending to walk
through the grounds to cool off, and it wasn't until
she was passing the administration block that she
realised it was raining. Several of the office staff
were staring out of their windows at her, no doubt
wondering what one of the nursing sisters was doing
in her uniform traipsing round the flowerbeds in the
pouring rain.

Hurriedly, with her head down, she made her way
to the nearest entrance that would take her back
into the factory. It happened to be a goods'
entrance, and as she pushed open the heavy doors
and slipped inside the deafening noise hit her—of

hammering and drilling and the drone of the hydraulic pumps that operated the floor levels together with the shouts of the men operating the overhead cranes.

She made her way across the factory floor and it was when she was nearly back at the occupational health centre that she heard a whistle. It was an appreciative whistle and one that Rachel recognised, for since she'd been working with five thousand men she had become well used to whistles of that nature.

Today, however, when she glanced up and saw two men high above her on a jig smiling and nudging each other, she simply fled back to the sanctuary of her office.

# CHAPTER FOUR

'WHAT'S this your mother tells me about Markham coming to work at OBEX?'

Rachel sighed. 'Yes, Dad, I'm afraid it's true.'

'I don't know how he's got the neck to come back to these parts.'

'I suppose it's because he comes from this area — his home is here. Oh, don't worry,' she added, catching sight of her father's expression, 'I'm not defending him — far from it — I was as angry as you when I knew he was back.'

It was the following weekend and Rachel was helping her father, who had just given the lawn its last cut before winter, to dispose of the grass cuttings on the compost heap at the bottom of the garden.

'I couldn't believe it when your mother told me.' Ken Stevens tipped up the wheelbarrow then stood back to rest for a moment. 'Has it been difficult for you at work?'

'Just a bit,' admitted Rachel but she refrained from saying exactly why. 'But the way I see it I've just got to get on with it, I don't have any choice.' She glanced up quickly. 'Jennifer doesn't know, does she?'

Her father shook his head. 'No, and I think it's best to keep it that way. Your mother mentioned

Family Day—do you think it'll be too much of a problem? Would it be better if we didn't come?'

'I don't think it need come to that. As I said to Mum, there will be thousands there and if David Markham is one of them it will just be a question of avoiding him. After all, I don't see why Jennifer should miss out on the one thing she's actually looking forward to just because of him.'

'My sentiments exactly,' said her father grimly, bending down to lift the wheelbarrow handles again. 'But on the other hand I don't want her upset either, and seeing him would be the one thing guaranteed to do just that.'

Rachel watched him as he tramped back through the fruit trees towards the house. Ken Stevens loved both his girls and Rachel knew it had taken him a long time to come to terms with Jennifer's illness; she doubted he would ever forgive David Markham for walking out on her at such a crucial time.

She herself had spent the remainder of the previous week keeping out of David's way as much as possible. It was difficult while they were actually in the centre, of course, but she made sure she didn't go for coffee or to the staff canteen at the same time as him and she'd avoided the social club completely. If there were rumours concerning herself and the new medical officer she wanted them quashed before they had a chance to spread.

She had even avoided the swimming-pool, for, much as she looked forward to and enjoyed her evening dips, she didn't want to give him any further opportunity to seek her company. She couldn't believe that what Greg Bradshaw had said was true and that David Markham was seriously interested in her, even though, she had to admit, there had been moments when she had wondered, but she wasn't prepared to take any chances.

By the middle of the following week, however, she was really missing her trips to the pool and she decided that on Wednesday afternoon, which was one of the afternoons when David wasn't at the factory, she would take a chance and go for a swim.

On Wednesday they had a quiet morning in the centre until just before lunch when two emergencies came in at virtually the same time. One was a young man from the shop-floor who'd got a metal splinter in his eye and the other was a secretary who had caught her heel in one of the open staircases and twisted her ankle.

While Nina was applying cold compresses to the swollen ankle, Rachel put drops into the man's eye.

'Were you using a face mask?' she asked.

'No. . .I didn't bother. . .I only had one bit to do on that section; it didn't seem worth it.'

'So did you use the eyewash equipment on the jig?'

'Yes, but it didn't make no difference.' As he shook his head his long hair parted and Rachel saw the gleam of an earring.

When she examined his eye she saw the splinter, a tiny coil of metal shaving which appeared to be sticking to the iris. It resisted her attempts to remove it and she asked the patient to wait while she asked the doctor to look at it.

After David had examined the patient he straightened up and said, 'I'm going to refer you to an eye specialist at the hospital as I'm afraid the metal particle may have become embedded and caused some damage. Sister will put a pad over your eye for the time being; I'll telephone the hospital and we'll arrange for someone to drive you over there.'

'I won't go blind, will I?' The young man looked startled that what he'd thought was just a speck in his eye was turning out to be something much more serious. David attempted to reassure him, and after he'd arranged for him to be seen in the casualty department of the local eye unit he asked the factory welfare officer, Louise Raymond, to take him over. As they left the centre, David turned to Rachel.

'I gather he wasn't wearing a mask?'

'That's right,' she replied. 'It's incredible, isn't it? After all our lectures, they still don't think accident prevention applies to them. I'm really not sure what else we can do.'

'Just keep hammering away,' David replied, then, glancing at the clock, he said, 'Good lord, is that the time? I must go.' He slipped off his white coat and a few minutes later he hurried from the centre.

'It's nice for some, working part-time, isn't it?' remarked Rachel to Nina.

'Doesn't he do anything else? When he isn't here, I mean?'

'I shouldn't think so; if he did — hospital clinics or

that sort of thing—he would have said, wouldn't he?'

'I suppose so, although. . .' Nina hesitated '. . .he's a bit of a mystery.'

'What do you mean?' Rachel stared at her.

'According to you, he's supposed to be such a hard man. . .'

'Yes, he is. . .'

'Well, that doesn't tie in with what I heard about him.'

'What have you heard?' Rachel frowned.

'That since he came back from Australia he's been living with his mother.'

'His mother!' Rachel's eyes widened in amazement. It was the last thing she would have expected of David Markham.

'That's what I heard. Did he live at home when he was engaged to your sister?'

Rachel shook her head. 'No, he had his own flat then.'

'Maybe he's just staying with his mother until he finds a place of his own.'

'Hmm, maybe,' replied Rachel thoughtfully, then, changing the subject, she said, 'I think I'll go to lunch now, then later this afternoon I want to get in a quick swim.'

When Rachel arrived at the pool the attendant came out of his office and smiled when he saw her. 'Oh, it's you, Sister; that's all right, I'm sure you can go in.'

She thought the remark was odd but before she had a chance to query it the attendant's phone rang and as he disappeared Rachel went on to the changing-rooms. It didn't take her long to change into her jade swimsuit and moments later she walked on to the poolside.

She had been expecting the pool to be almost empty at that time of day and was surprised to see that there were about a dozen or so people in the water. The smell of chlorine engulfed her and someone suddenly blew a whistle, the sound echoing in the large enclosed area. She stared at the people in the pool, who had all seemed to respond to the whistle and were looking at someone who stood at the poolside, someone obscured from Rachel's vision by the attendant's tall chair.

She frowned; there was something about the people in the water that made her look more closely. Then she realised that they weren't employees of OBEX and that they all appeared to be handicapped in some way.

A middle-aged woman with cropped grey hair was in the pool, apparently supervising the party, but even as Rachel watched in amazement the figure behind the chair stepped forward and with a shock she saw it was David.

'Rachel!' The pleasure in his surprised look was only too apparent. 'Have you come to join us?'

Her first instinct was to turn and walk straight back to the changing-rooms; after all, hadn't she come here at the one time when she'd thought David

Markham was safely out of the way? But something about his smile made her hesitate, then someone in the pool called out, 'Hello, Rachel.'

She turned and saw it was a young man quite obviously afflicted by Down's syndrome who had called her. Then another of the party called her name, a girl this time, and within seconds it was taken up by everyone in the pool.

'Hello, Rachel,' they chorused.

'Hello.' She smiled at them.

'Are you joining us for a swim?' asked David in a loud voice.

Again what he said was repeated by everyone else and he grinned. Rachel sighed and shook her head slightly then with a little shrug she sat down on the side of the pool and dangled her legs in the water. Immediately she was surrounded by the other occupants of the pool, who crowded around her, laughing and urging her right into the water and ignoring the grey-haired woman who was trying to keep them under control.

As she slipped into the water beside them Rachel was aware that David had thrown a large orange ball into the pool before jumping in himself, and within seconds she found herself part of a noisy, boisterous game of water hand-ball.

The group, obviously delighted at having someone new in their midst, constantly called her name and it seemed to Rachel that every one of them wanted to throw the ball to her while she, infected by their enthusiasm, was only too happy to join in. She quickly realised that the majority of them seemed to have Down's syndrome while the disabilities of the others seemed to range from mild cerebral palsy to a spastic condition, these latter demanding the most attention and help from David and the woman who was with them.

In spite of her earlier misgivings at finding David in the pool, Rachel, still mindful of his pleasure when he had caught sight of her, soon began to enjoy herself and was disappointed when all too soon David blew the whistle again and said it was time to get out of the water.

She expected arguments, but there were none as the group obeyed David instantly, the more able-bodied standing quietly by the poolside while David, the woman, who she found out was called Sybil, and the pool attendant helped the more severely disabled out of the water and into wheelchairs.

Rachel too climbed out of the pool, not having the heart to carry on swimming now that the others had finished. While she changed, she could hear the others laughing and singing and when she emerged from the changing-room she found them all in the foyer waiting for her to emerge. A minibus with the words 'Conway House' emblazoned across its side stood at the entrance, its driver talking to Sybil and David.

As David caught sight of her he left the other two and came back into the foyer.

'They wouldn't go without saying goodbye,' he explained.

The next moment Rachel was surrounded again as with many hugs and cuddles the group took their leave of their new friend and finally filed into the minibus, where they lined the windows, smiling and waving.

'You've made their day,' commented David, who stood beside her, watching, as Alf, the driver, fastened the doors. 'They love making a new friend. Trouble is, they'll expect to see you here the next time they come.'

'Do they come regularly?' She shot him a surprised look as they both waved at the moving minibus.

'This is only their second time,' he replied. 'But yes, it seems to be working well, so they will be coming regularly.'

As the minibus disappeared out of the main gates they turned and went back into the foyer.

'Let me buy you a drink,' he said easily.

'No,' she replied quickly, mindful of the last time. 'No, really,' she added, catching sight of his surprised expression.

'Oh, come on, it's the least I can do after your help.'

Rachel found herself following him into the social club and a few minutes later when they were both seated with their drinks in the same window-seat where they had sat before she said, 'So what's your connection with Conway House?'

'I work there,' he replied simply, and when he saw

her astonished expression he set his glass down and laughed.

'Didn't you know? I thought I'd mentioned it. I work there when I'm not here.'

She stared at him. 'But I thought. . .I thought. . . oh, I don't know quite what I thought. . .' She trailed off helplessly.

'I'll tell you what you thought: you thought I only worked part-time and the rest of the time I just loafed around—that's it, isn't it?'

'Well. . .I. . .'

'Go on, admit it.' He grinned, teasing her now, and Rachel felt the colour rise to her cheeks. 'I heard you say as much in the centre one day.'

She swallowed, then, setting her own glass down, she took a deep breath. 'So why Conway House?' she asked in a desperate attempt to steer the conversation away from herself.

He shrugged. 'Why not? I love working with handicapped people; I did similar work in Australia in my spare time and, you have to admit, it does make a pleasant change from accidents and medicals.'

She stared at him as he sipped his lager, thinking it was a shame his compassion for handicapped people hadn't extended to her sister when she had most needed him. But maybe his interest had arisen since—from guilt.

She was about to ask him why the party had been using the OBEX pool when, as if he could read her thoughts, he said, 'I used to take them to the public swimming-pool in town, but it gets so crowded that some of them used to get frightened. I realised there were periods of time when this pool is hardly used, so I approached the management and asked if I could bring parties of residents here from Conway House. They were only too happy to oblige, but we decided to keep the sessions private.'

'That's why the attendant said he supposed it would be all right for me to go in,' said Rachel. 'I thought it sounded odd at the time; now I know why.'

They were silent for a moment, then David said, 'Have you ever visited Conway House?'

She shook her head. 'No, I've heard about it, of course, but I've never been there.'

'In that case you must come over some time and let me show you around. It's a marvellous place. And, of course, you must make sure you're here the next time we come swimming.' He smiled and his eyes met hers. 'You're the first person they'll ask for, I can assure you.'

For a long moment Rachel found she was unable to look away from that cool, slightly amused stare. Five minutes later, however, she became only too aware of other members of staff who were trickling into the social club as their shift ended and suddenly, mindful of the interpretation that had been put on her being with David Markham on the last occasion they had visited the club, she finished her drink and stood up.

'I really must be going,' she said.

'Why?' He stared up at her.

'I beg your pardon?'

'I asked why you had to be going.'

'Well. . .I have things to do. . .I have to go home. . .' she floundered.

'Sit down, Rachel.'

Her eyes widened. 'What?'

'I said sit down,' he repeated. 'I can't understand why you always seem to be in such a tearing hurry; why don't you just relax for five minutes and sit down?'

She stared at him for a further moment, then meekly she obeyed and he smiled.

'That's better. You don't have anyone to rush home to—or do you?' he asked, raising his eyebrows.

Quickly she shook her head. 'No, no, I don't.'

He sat back in his chair and surveyed her. 'I must admit I find it hard to believe that you don't have someone waiting for you.'

'Well, I don't and that's that.' She gave a short laugh, still uncomfortably embarrassed by the turn the situation had taken.

'So you're telling me there's no one important in your life. Has that always been so?'

'I didn't say that.'

'So there was someone once?'

She gave a slight shrug. 'There might have been.' She had no intention of telling him about Ian White, the medical registrar she had dated for over a year and who she had once thought might have come to mean much more in her life. Instead, she felt faintly annoyed at the boldness of his questions and decided to turn the tables.

'And what about you?' She tried to make it sound casual but was aware that her tone had risen slightly.

'Me?' He sounded surprised, as if it were perfectly acceptable for him to be questioning her, but not the other way round.

'Yes.' She persisted now, goaded by his manner, 'Is there anyone important in your life now?'

For a moment she thought he wasn't going to answer as he stared at his glass, then slowly he raised his eyes to hers. 'No,' he said quietly, 'there isn't anyone important in my life at present.'

For a moment Rachel was shocked by the expression in his eyes, for it was one of pain. Then she found herself concluding that her earlier assumption had probably been correct and that there had indeed been someone in Australia, someone who had caused him to return to England in a hurry.

The incident with the residents from Conway House seemed to have struck a note of rapport between Rachel and David and during the following week their working relationship seemed much less strained.

News of his work with the handicapped also leaked out at the centre and it became common knowledge that he was using the OBEX swimming-pool.

One morning during coffee-break, Rachel found

Nina and Louise apparently discussing David, who had gone to a meeting.

'To think we thought he only worked part-time,' Nina was saying as Rachel came into the room.

Louise nodded. 'I know, I used to think he skived off and all the time he was going on to Conway House to work. And now he's started bringing the residents here — have you seen him with them?' She glanced at the other two and, not waiting for a reply, she went on, 'He's so caring, he treats them as if they're his personal friends. . .' She glanced up as the secretary put her head round the door. 'Oh, Michelle, are you looking for me? I'll be right with you.'

Nina looked at Rachel as Louise hurried from the room. 'That's not quite the picture you had of our Dr David Markham, is it, Rachel?' she said quietly.

'It certainly isn't; in fact I'm beginning to wonder if this is the same man who hurt my sister so badly——' She broke off abruptly as the emergency alarm phone began ringing.

She grabbed the receiver while Nina stood up, anticipating trouble, and watching Rachel as she took the call.

'What is it?' she asked anxiously as Rachel pressed the button and immediately began re-dialling.

'An accident on one of the jigs. A man's fallen through,' she said abruptly.

# CHAPTER FIVE

RACHEL asked the switchboard to page Dr Markham in his meeting, then she sent for Greg and the factory ambulance. Within minutes she and Nina were in the ambulance being driven across the vast factory to the section where the accident had taken place.

As they climbed from the back of the ambulance Rachel was met by the foreman of that particular section, who informed her that the man had fallen from the top of the jig to the second section.

'Our first-aider is with him, but he's in a very awkward position—is the doctor with you?'

'He's on his way,' replied Rachel, hoping that David wouldn't be long. She instructed Nina to radio for the county ambulance before climbing the stairs to the first floor of the jig and following the foreman along the boards for about twenty yards until they were able to see the injured man. He appeared to be wedged between the two sections of flooring; his body was twisted, his face very pale but his eyes were open and he was fully conscious. Rachel crawled into the confined space beside him, and with a little jolt she saw it was Len Seager, the man who had been having alcohol-related problems.

'Hello, Len,' she said quietly. 'Are you in a lot of pain?'

He managed a faint smile. 'Hello, Sister, bloody silly thing to do, wasn't it? I just slipped, next thing I knew I was down here; funny thing is, it don't really hurt—I can't feel much at all.'

Rachel glanced at the first-aider who was holding Len's head. The man raised his eyebrows, then said, 'I've been trying to keep him as still as possible, Sister.'

'Yes, well done. Did you see the accident?'

'No.' The man shook his head. 'Jimmy Warren did, though.'

Rachel turned in the cramped space and saw that someone else had joined them on the jig.

'What do we have, Rachel?' The quiet, controlled voice filled her with relief and she scrambled out on to the jig to join David.

'It's Len Seager,' she said softly, noting the flicker of recognition in David's eyes at mention of the man's name. 'He apparently slipped and has fallen between the floors.' She lowered her voice even more so that the injured man wouldn't hear. 'I would say he has spinal injuries. It's going to be very difficult to get him out.'

'Are the county boys on their way?'

She nodded, then Nina appeared on the jig beside them, carrying a neck collar.

From that moment David took absolute control and while Rachel crawled back into the space and fitted the collar, immobilising Len as much as possible, he administered a pethidine injection, all the time talking and trying to reassure the patient.

After what seem an eternity, but which in reality could only have been about fifteen minutes, the paramedics from the county ambulance service arrived, and under David's supervision the serious business of trying to lift Len out began. At last, with Greg's help, they managed to get him on to a stretcher to which he was firmly secured with nylon strapping so that it was virtually impossible for him to move, then the stretcher was carefully lifted down from the jig and into the waiting ambulance.

Len Seager had been conscious throughout the entire rescue operation and as Rachel joined him briefly in the back of the ambulance and covered him with an extra blanket he managed another smile.

'Caused a bit of excitement, haven't I, Sister?' he joked.

'You certainly have, Len,' she replied.

'Are you coming with me?' Suddenly he looked anxious.

'No, Len, not me,' replied Rachel, 'but Sister Clarey will go to the hospital with you. Is there anyone we can contact for you?'

'No, not really,' he replied, and Rachel remembered that his wife had left him, then as she turned to go he suddenly spoke again. 'Oh, yes, there is someone,' he said and when Rachel paused he added, 'My parrot.'

'Your parrot?' Rachel stopped and looked back at him in surprise.

'Yes, he'll want feeding. Could someone tell my next-door neighbour, Mrs Timms? She's got a key.'

'Of course, Len, don't worry,' said Rachel gently, finding unexpectedly that she had a lump in her throat at the thought of Len having no one in his life but his parrot.

'I feel as if we failed that man somewhere,' she said a little later as together with David and Martin Foulds she watched the ambulance leave the factory.

Neither David nor the superintendent replied, but Rachel knew from their expressions that they agreed with her. With a sigh, she said, 'I'd better get back and fill out an accident report — I would imagine there will be quite an enquiry into this one.' She turned to go then paused at a shout from the foreman.

'Sister, it's Jimmy Warren; he's in a bit of a state.'

'All right.' Rachel glanced at David. 'It'll be shock; we'll take him back to the centre with us.'

Jimmy Warren was indeed in a state of shock at what he had witnessed and Rachel knew that he would require post-incident-trauma counselling.

Her detailed report, which began with the call she had taken reporting the accident, included her call to the county ambulance, accounts from other men on the shop-floor, the foreman's version of what happened, first aid given, and on-the-spot treatment that had been administered by the factory medical team. The report even included the fact that she had advised the factory welfare officer, on the patient's instructions, to contact his neighbour.

When it was confirmed that Len Seager had broken his neck a meeting was called with all relevant parties to discuss the case. Martin Foulds reported that Len's alcohol problem had been previously discussed with the medical team and it had been decided to try to arrange counselling for him.

'The trouble was, Len himself refused to accept that he had a problem,' said Martin. 'I had arranged with Sister Stevens that on the next occasion that Len presented with either a hangover or a stomach upset I would refer him to the occupational health centre where they would suggest counselling, as I believed Len was becoming a danger to himself and everyone else.'

'And wasn't this done?' This question came from the management representative who was attending the meeting.

'The opportunity didn't arise,' replied Martin. 'In fact, for a while there Len seemed much better. He wasn't even late for work, let alone under the influence of drink, so I could hardly suggest counselling in those circumstances.'

'And what about on the morning of the accident?' asked David.

'I hadn't seen him,' admitted Martin and turned to the foreman.

'He seemed quiet and rather withdrawn that morning, but he very often was so I didn't take too much notice. Jimmy Warren, who was apparently the only witness actually to see him fall, said he also hadn't noticed anything untoward about Len that morning.'

'I still think we failed him,' said Rachel to David when the meeting was over.

'What do you think we could have done?'

'I'm not absolutely sure, but I think our suggestion of counselling came far too late. Here we had a man who we knew had serious problems that constituted a danger to himself and others, and we sat back, simply because we were waiting for him to admit he had a problem.'

'So what in your opinion is the solution?'

'I think it has something to do with the word counselling; people seem afraid of it — maybe it conjures up the wrong image — that they feel they've failed in some way if they have to resort to counselling. I'd like to set up a different sort of help-line, something informal and friendly where the employees won't be afraid to discuss their problems.'

'It sounds a bit idealistic,' remarked David, 'but I'm with you one hundred per cent.'

She stared at him. Somehow she'd been expecting resistance, something she had frequently encountered with Graham Rowell whenever she had attempted anything new, and it came as a shock to find that she and David Markham were on the same wavelength.

Almost immediately they began working out the details of their new counselling service — or, as they preferred to call it, their chat-line — and how and where they could fit it into their already busy schedule. The other members of the medical team seemed equally enthusiastic, with even the night charge nurse, Alan Hill, joining in.

'You'd be amazed how many workers are prepared to offload their problems during the witching hour,' he said when he was told of the project.

Rachel was relieved that everything seemed to be running so smoothly, not only with the setting up of the chat-line but with the new, easygoing atmosphere in the centre. Then one afternoon Louise Raymond visited Len Seager in hospital and reported back to the rest of the team.

'He's quadriplegic,' she said quietly.

'What does that mean?' asked Michelle, who was checking records.

'No movement from the neck down.' It was David who gave the grim reply to the secretary's question.

The girl stared at him. 'God, how awful! The poor man, whatever will he do?'

'He'll have to have residential care,' said Nina.

'Maybe Conway House would be suitable,' mused David.

'Isn't that only for the mentally handicapped?' asked Nina curiously.

'No.' It was David who replied to Nina's question. 'They take any handicapped person—mentally or physically, either long term, or short term to give carers a break.'

'Do they?' said Rachel thoughtfully.

'Were you thinking about your sister, Rachel?' asked Nina.

Rachel hesitated, then nodded. She *had* been thinking of Jennifer, but she hadn't wanted to say as much in front of David. His reaction, however, was instantaneous. 'I didn't realise Jennifer had reached the stage where she might need residential care.'

'It would only be occasional and short term—purely to give my parents a break.' She was unable to disguise the bleak note that had entered her voice. There was silence for a moment then Nina murmured an excuse and hurried away, no doubt embarrassed by the turn the conversation had taken. Rachel said, 'I'm not sure that Conway House would be suitable, though. . .'

'There's only one way to find out,' said David smoothly, 'and that's to go and see for yourself. Tell you what,' he went on, not giving Rachel a chance to speak, 'I have to go this evening; why don't you come with me?'

'Well. . .I. . .' She faltered, desperately searching for some excuse.

'The only problem is, my car is going in for a service, so maybe you could do me a favour and give me a lift there? I'm living at Brooklands—you know where that is, don't you? Shall we say about seven o'clock?' He smiled and moved swiftly out of her office, leaving Rachel staring after him in exasperation. Not only had he managed to manipulate her into going with him to Conway House but also into picking him up from his home and taking him there as well!

One thing he had confirmed, though, was the fact

that he was living at Brooklands, his mother's home, so Nina had been quite right in that respect, but it still left Rachel wondering why.

David had been right when he'd said that Rachel knew the whereabouts of Brooklands, for she had been there with her parents and her sister shortly after David and Jennifer's engagement had been announced.

It was a gabled Victorian house set behind a high red brick wall in the heart of the city and as Rachel drew on to the gravel forecourt she sat for a moment admiring the mass of copper beeches that surrounded the house. The autumn evenings had started to draw in, there was a slight chill in the air, and as Rachel stepped from her car she was glad she'd worn her thick navy fisherman's sweater over her jeans.

As she rang the ornate brass doorbell and waited she caught the acrid scent of burning leaves from a garden bonfire, then a nearby church clock chimed the hour.

She was about to ring the bell again when the door was opened by David's mother. Rachel hadn't seen Irene Markham for five years but she was shocked by how much older she looked. Tall and elegant, her silver-grey hair styled into a smooth bob, she stood in the doorway and coolly surveyed Rachel with the same steady, grey-eyed gaze of her son.

'Good evening, Rachel. David said you would be

calling. Would you like to come in? He's on the telephone at the moment.' She spoke in short, clipped sentences and stood aside for Rachel to enter the house.

'Hello, Mrs Markham.' Feeling decidedly uncomfortable at the older woman's frosty manner, Rachel reluctantly followed her into the sitting-room hoping that David wasn't going to be long.

The room was elegant and, although comfortably and expensively furnished, was free from clutter and without any of the personal touches that for Rachel made a house a home. Irene Markham indicated for her to sit down and she perched on the very edge of an upright chair suddenly feeling quite miserable and wishing she hadn't come.

'I trust your parents are well?'

'Yes, quite well, thank you.' Rachel waited for the older woman to mention Jennifer.

Instead she said, 'David tells me you are also working in industry. Have you been at OBEX long?'

'About two years.'

'And you have no plans to go back into general nursing?'

'Not at the moment. . .'

'I was disappointed when David left surgery; I had always imagined he would follow in his father's footsteps—but, as we know, circumstances decreed otherwise.'

Rachel stiffened. It sounded as if this woman was blaming Jennifer for falling ill, instead of her precious son for running out on the situation.

Angrily she opened her mouth to protest but at that moment the door opened and David appeared.

He glanced quickly at his mother then back to Rachel again. 'Sorry to keep you waiting. Shall we go?'

Rachel was still fuming when David took his place beside her in her car. Without a backward glance at Brooklands or the woman who stood watching them from the doorway, she pulled out into the flow of traffic, her tyres squealing on the loose gravel drive.

Tight-lipped, she drove in silence, keeping her eyes firmly on the road, but as they sat at red traffic-lights waiting for them to change she couldn't keep silent any longer.

'Your mother seems bitter about something,' she said sharply.

David shrugged. 'That's mothers for you. And, from what I hear, mothers of sons are the worst.'

'But I don't understand why she should feel. . .' Rachel jumped as David nudged her. 'What?' She looked up and saw that the lights had changed to green and as the car behind her sounded its horn she let out the clutch too quickly and the car lurched forward.

'I thought,' he said calmly a few minutes later, 'we had agreed not to discuss the past.'

'Yes, we had,' she admitted, 'but. . .'

'And I thought that, because we had agreed to that, our working relationship had improved.'

'Yes. . .'

'In that case I suggest we stick to it, because I

have the strong feeling that if we start digging up what happened five years ago we will start arguing, and that won't help anybody.'

Rachel was silent, then she nodded. 'Yes, all right,' she agreed at last.

Ten minutes later she drove into the main entrance of Conway House and gradually she felt her anger ebb away.

David introduced her to the warden, then they made their way to the residents' common-room where Rachel was given a rapturous welcome by her new friends, in particular by a young Down's syndrome woman called Belinda whose delight at seeing her again was only too apparent.

They were given tea and biscuits, invited to watch a favourite soap opera on the television, then made to listen to current hits from the charts played for them by a young man called Danny on his ghetto-blaster.

The common-room was large and comfortably furnished and at the far end included pool tables, dartboards and table tennis. It was bright, with house-plants, posters of pop stars and cartoons and in one corner there even appeared to be a hamster or a gerbil in a cage, but as Rachel looked around she caught David watching her carefully.

'What are you thinking?' he asked quietly.

'That it's very nice and that everyone seems very happy.'

'But. . .?'

'What do you mean, but?' She threw him a quick glance.

'It sounded as if a but was going to follow that statement.' When Rachel remained silent, he said, 'What you are really thinking is that you can't imagine Jennifer fitting in here, aren't you?'

Still she didn't reply, unsure how to put her thoughts into words, for she had indeed had doubts about her sister adapting to the environment.

'In a moment I want to take you across to the Rosemount wing. This section is for permanent residents; I brought you here first because if it had got out that you had been here and hadn't seen this lot my life wouldn't have been worth living. They haven't stopped talking about you since that day in the pool.'

After lengthy farewells Rachel followed David across the grounds to the Rosemount wing, which turned out to be a new building that had only recently been opened. As they entered they could hear someone playing a cello.

'The Rosemount is primarily for short-term patients, people like Jennifer who can't manage alone and who need respite care.'

The rooms, Rachel noticed, were mainly single but a few were shared. 'Some patients like privacy,' explained David, 'but we find that others need company. Most of our short-term patients are suffering from diseases such as muscular dystrophy, motor neurone disease, Huntington's chorea or multiple sclerosis. It has been proved that even a short stay helps not only the carers, but the patients, who greatly benefit from a change of scenery and the use of the many facilities we have here.' He turned to Rachel as he finished speaking. 'Do you think that something like this might be the answer for Jennifer — and for your parents?'

She nodded slowly. 'It could well be. I was dubious at first because since her illness Jennifer has become a very private person and I don't think she would have liked all the hubbub over in the other section; but here ——' she glanced round at the softly decorated walls, the strategically placed water-colours and the subdued lighting '— here, I think, could well be the answer.'

'What do you think would be your parents' reaction?'

'I'm not sure,' said Rachel slowly. 'They have always said they will care for Jennifer completely, and until now they've only allowed me to stand in for them, but it's taking its toll. My mother had to give up teaching to be at home all the time, and she's beginning to look very tired, while my father seems to have aged ten years.'

'It is a tremendous responsibility caring for a handicapped person.'

Rachel glanced quickly at David, wondering if that statement was going to be the closest he came to admitting that the care of Jennifer should have been his responsibility and that he had opted out, but his expression remained impassive, giving away nothing of his feelings.

'The situation has been eased slightly for my parents since a community nurse has been visiting Jennifer, but I must admit I'd rapidly been coming to the conclusion that something else would be needed very soon. The difficult part will be getting them to accept it.'

'Could I help there?' The question appeared casual but the intention sounded genuine enough.

'What do you mean?' Rachel frowned.

'Well, would you like me to approach your parents and suggest Jennifer coming to Rosemount?'

'Oh, no,' said Rachel quickly — too quickly.

He raised his eyebrows. 'I simply thought it might help. . .'

'I know, I know, David, but I don't think that would be a very good idea.' She had a sudden vision of her father's face if he found David Markham on his doorstep and the ensuing battle when he found out what his proposals were. 'I think,' she went on hurriedly, 'that it might be best if it were to come from me. As it is. . .' She trailed off, uncertain how to continue.

He gave her a keen glance. 'Were you about to say, as it is there will be problems when your parents and Jennifer know I'm working here?' When Rachel remained silent he went on, 'That needn't be a problem; my work is almost entirely with the permanent residents — in fact I hardly ever come over here to the Rosemount wing.'

Still she hesitated and at last he said, 'Think about it, talk to your parents and to Jennifer and see what the reaction is. It could be the answer for them all, just as it could be the answer for Len Seager.'

'Oh, yes,' she replied, relieved that the conversation had switched to Len, 'I think it would be ideal for Len; I'll talk to Louise Raymond in the morning and see if we can arrange anything through the company—it's the least we can do for him.'

David nodded then said, 'Well, if you've seen enough, shall we be going?'

She nodded and followed him from the Rosemount wing and across the grounds to her car.

Then as he climbed into the passenger seat he said, 'Would you like to come back for coffee?'

Desperately she sought for an excuse, anything not to have to face his mother's frosty manner again, but before she could think of anything he said, 'On second thoughts, I have a better idea.'

She turned and glanced at him enquiringly.

'How about we go for a bite to eat somewhere?'

Rachel was about to protest—this sounded like dangerous ground—but somehow it seemed the lesser of two evils and as she turned the key in the ignition she felt a flutter of excitement and she knew, deep down, that she wanted to go with him.

# CHAPTER SIX

RACHEL drove to an old inn beside the canal that had once been the haunt of the bargees and their families who travelled the canals. They found an alcove beside a vast inglenook fireplace hung with horse brasses and halters, reminders of the working barge horses, and after ordering steak and salad they sipped lager from pewter tankards.

'So what do you actually do at Conway House?' Rachel asked after a while. 'Are you there as a doctor?'

'Partly.' He smiled. 'But mostly I simply help with the residents — you know, organise activities and outings, that sort of thing. It takes a tremendous amount of organisation.'

'I'm sure it does, but it must be very worthwhile; they all adore you.'

He smiled. 'You've noticed. But I shall have to watch out; I think I have a rival for their affections. They won't give me a minute's peace tomorrow now that you've been to the centre.'

'What do you mean?' Rachel laughed but was secretly pleased at her apparent popularity.

'They'll be pestering me to know when they can see you again. . .' He set his glass down and casually said, 'What shall I tell them?'

'I don't know.' She shrugged. 'When are they coming swimming again?'

'Not until next week—that will seem like a lifetime away to them; but I am taking some of them out on Sunday up to Pelham Woods for a walk; how about joining us?'

'Well. . .' She hesitated.

'Or are you helping with Jennifer on Sunday?'

'No, I shall be going there on Saturday. . .'

'So, it's a date, then?' His grey eyes met hers and she was forced to smile at the gleam of amusement she saw there.

'Yes, all right,' she said at last, 'it's a date.'

Anything less like a conventional date she couldn't imagine, but she was rapidly beginning to realise that David Markham was not a conventional sort of person, and besides, she told herself firmly, even if he had been, he was the last person she would arrange a date with.

It wasn't until they were halfway through their meal that David suddenly said, 'Do you ever see any of the old crowd from St Clare's?'

'Sometimes,' she admitted. 'The girls I trained with occasionally have a get-together.'

'What about the medical staff—do you ever see any of them?' He said it casually but Rachel threw him a sharp glance. Had he heard about her romance with Ian White, the junior registrar?

'No, not really,' she replied guardedly. 'But then I wouldn't; I didn't know many of the medical team—they were Jennifer's friends rather than mine.'

He nodded then asked, 'Does she see any of them now?'

'No. I believe some of them visited at first, but it gradually dwindled—even Sonia and Paul Mason, whom she was very friendly with, stopped visiting. Do you remember them? He was senior gynae reg and his wife was a physiotherapist. . .'

'Yes, I remember.' His reply was curt. 'What happened to them?'

'I've no idea. I think they moved down south. . . I don't think Jennifer even hears from them any more. . .it's sad really how people just don't want to know. . .' She trailed off, suddenly aware of whom she was speaking to.

Then as David got up to order another drink she found that her anger towards him was dwindling; after all, she could hardly accuse him of being uncaring when she was only too aware of the caring nature of his activities. She found herself watching him as he carried their drinks back to the table, the easy way he moved, his casual dress, his ready smile, and in spite of her previous reservations she realised she was liking what she saw.

She had dismissed as rubbish Nina's allegations that the men thought he was interested in her, but she had to admit he was good company, and for the next half-hour he entertained her with stories of his work in Australia, of the people he'd met and of his excursions into the bush and to the Great Barrier Reef.

All too soon it was time to go and it was almost reluctantly that she drove him back to Brooklands. She parked outside the high brick wall rather than driving on to the forecourt, and as if he sensed her reluctance to enter the house again he didn't attempt to invite her inside — but neither did he make any attempt to get out of the car, and they sat in silence in the light from an overhead street-lamp.

A keen breeze had sprung up and they watched as it chased fallen leaves along the pavement, blowing them into little heaps against the red brick wall.

Then gradually, in the stillness and the silence, Rachel became very aware of David's closeness in the confined space of the car and her heart began beating very fast.

In the end, it was she who broke the silence that was threatening to overwhelm them.

'Thank you for the meal,' she said, and her voice sounded breathless as if she'd been running.

'Don't mention it,' he replied softly. 'Believe me, it was my pleasure.' He turned towards her then and she stiffened, her nerves suddenly stretched to breaking-point.

He moved his hand and gently touched one of hers that was tightly gripping the steering-wheel. That was all, the slightest touch of his fingers on hers, but she was reminded of that other time he had touched her, when he'd helped her out of the pool, and now, as then, something inside her responded to his touch. Just for a moment she remained very still, her senses taut, enjoying the light caress of his fingers. Surely there was no harm in this, just sitting here in her car with David Markham, a man whom after all, she'd known for years. A man who'd once been engaged to her sister.

Common sense returned quite suddenly, hitting her like some tangible thing, and she jumped, an involuntary reaction as if she'd been bitten.

Startled, he drew back, and was still for a few seconds, watching her as she battled with her thoughts, then with a barely audible sigh he said, 'What is it, Rachel? What's wrong?'

'Nothing,' she mumbled. 'I think you'd better go, David.'

'But. . .'

'No, I mean it.'

'Very well. If that's what you want. Goodnight, Rachel.'

Then he was gone, out of the car and through the gates of Brooklands without looking back.

Rachel sat for a moment as the wind playfully tossed a handful of leaves on to the bonnet of the car, and as she turned the key in the ignition she realised she was trembling.

The following morning, after a troubled night of confused dreams, Rachel broached the possibility to Louise Raymond of Len Seager going to Conway House. 'I think it'll be the ideal place for him when he's eventually discharged from hospital,' she said.

'Do you think you could look into the necessary arrangements that would have to be made, Louise?'

'Of course.' The welfare officer smiled. 'I'll be only too pleased to help get something sorted out for poor old Len; life isn't exactly going to be easy for him. The union representative is looking into the case to see if the company have a negligence claim to answer, but at the moment it rather looks as if it was entirely Len's fault. If that proves to be the case it seems unlikely that he would even be able to claim compensation.'

'Conway House is run by a charity so finance shouldn't be a problem,' said Rachel thoughtfully, then added, 'And I wouldn't have thought there would be any question of Len's not being a deserving case. He doesn't even have any family, does he, Louise?'

Louise shook her head. 'No, he's completely alone.'

They were silent for a moment, Rachel trying to contemplate what it must be like to be entirely alone in the world, then, as a sudden thought hit her she glanced up. 'What happened to his parrot?'

'His neighbour is looking after it at the moment but I don't think she'll be prepared to keep it indefinitely. Do you think he would be able to take it with him if he goes to Conway House?'

'I would hope so,' replied Rachel. 'Apparently it's the policy of Conway House to be as much like home for its residents as it can.'

'Have you been there?' asked Louise.

Rachel nodded. 'Yes, I went there last night. I was most impressed.'

'Did Dr Markham take you?' The question was casual but Rachel thought she detected a flicker of interest in Louise's blue eyes and she wondered if the stories about herself and David had reached the welfare office yet or whether she was simply becoming paranoid where he was concerned.

'Yes,' she replied lightly. 'Dr Markham did take me, but he was the obvious person to do so, especially as he works there.'

'You said you were impressed with the place; do you think it's going to be suitable for your sister as well as for Len Seager?'

'I'm not sure about that,' said Rachel. 'My parents are the ones who need to be convinced, and I'm not sure that's going to be an easy task.'

'You mean because they want to care for your sister on their own?'

'Something like that, yes.' Rachel refrained from adding that the presence of David Markham at Conway House could well be the deciding factor as to whether Jennifer went there or not. Nina Clarey was the only one at OBEX who knew that her sister had once been engaged to the medical officer, and Rachel was anxious to keep it that way.

Later that same morning Rachel saw Jimmy Warren for a counselling session. The first thing she noticed about him as he walked into her office was that he looked tired and rather drawn.

'Come and sit down, Jimmy.' She indicated a chair alongside her own.

'I'm not really sure why I'm here,' mumbled Jimmy. He was a man in his late twenties, dark and thin with a sallow complexion. He had worked for OBEX since leaving school.

'You suffered quite badly from shock after Len's accident.'

'Yeah, I know all that.' He sounded impatient. 'But I'm OK now. I don't want the lads thinking I'm some sort of wimp, that can't cope with a bit of shock.'

'I'm sure they wouldn't think that, Jimmy.'

'You don't know them, Sister,' he said darkly, 'and if they're not thinking that then they'll say I'm skiving or only coming over here to chat up the nurses.'

'Well, if you're sure you're not suffering from any after-effects from the accident, I won't keep you any longer,' said Rachel with a brief smile, then as Jimmy stood up to leave she said casually, 'By the way, have you been to see Len?'

He had turned to the door, but he paused with one hand on the handle, and without turning round he said, 'No, I haven't.'

'Oh? I'm sure he'd be glad to see you. Haven't you two always worked together?'

'Yeah,' he nodded, 'Len taught me my trade.' He hesitated and Rachel remained silent, then slowly he turned his head to look at her. 'He's in a pretty bad way, isn't he, Sister?'

'Yes, Jimmy, he is. He has virtually no movement in any of his limbs.'

Jimmy was silent for a moment, then he said, 'What sort of thing did you mean when you asked if I was suffering any after-effects?'

'Well, anything unusual like loss of appetite, headaches, panic attacks. . .'

He hesitated, then, his embarrassment clearly showing, he asked, 'Would you include nightmares in that list?'

'I think, Jimmy, you'd better come and sit down again,' said Rachel quietly. She watched him carefully as he moved away from the door and came and sat down. 'When did these nightmares start?'

'Practically right away, after the accident.'

'And do you have them every night?'

'More or less.'

'What form do they take?'

He frowned and Rachel carefully re-phrased the question. 'Are the dreams always the same?'

'Not always.' He fidgeted on his chair as if even thinking of them caused agitation. 'But they always end up the same—I see that terrible expression on Len's face as he fell—then I hear the thud as he hits the floor—then I wake up in a cold sweat. And that's my lot; I don't go back to sleep again after that.' He was silent for a moment, staring at the floor, then he looked up at Rachel again. 'So that's about it, Sister—not a lot you can do about that, is there? Not unless you have some magic pill for nightmares.'

'No, Jimmy, I don't have that, but I do think it might be a good idea if you were to visit Len.'

'I don't see how that's going to cure my nightmares. . .'

'Maybe not but I think both you and Len might benefit by talking about what happened that morning; after all, apparently you were the only one who actually saw him fall. So how about it? Why don't you pop along to the hospital one night and pay Len a visit? I don't think he has that many visitors and I feel we should give him all the support we can.'

When Jimmy didn't answer Rachel leaned forward. 'What is it, Jimmy? What's wrong? Don't you want to visit Len?' She noticed a thin line of sweat on his upper lip as he struggled to speak.

'I'm not sure that I can, Sister. I've always had this thing about hospitals, you see. I hate the places and I don't think I could handle going in there and seeing Len smashed up like that. He's been a really decent bloke to me and I reckon he's had a rough deal, what with that wife of his clearing off and now this. . .'

'Isn't that all the more reason to give him your support?'

Still he hesitated and at that moment there came a tap at Rachel's door and David put his head round. Her heart leapt at the sight of him.

'Oh, sorry, Sister,' he said, 'I didn't know you had anyone with you.'

'It's all right, Dr Markham,' she replied, then in a sudden flash of inspiration, and hoping that David would realise what she meant, she said, 'Jimmy and I were just discussing visiting Len Seager in hospital. Jimmy's not too keen on going on his own. We were planning a visit, weren't we? I'm sure it could be arranged for Jimmy to come with us.'

'I don't see why not,' said David easily.

Instinctively Rachel knew he had at least partly understood the situation. 'Would that suit you, Jimmy?' she asked quietly.

'Yeah, I think it might.' He stood up again. 'I'd better be getting back or the foreman will be giving me the sack.'

'OK, Jimmy. We'll let you know about the visit.'

They watched as he left the room then David turned to Rachel. 'What was all that about? Did I give the right answer?'

'You did. Thanks. Jimmy Warren is experiencing stress trauma and I had suggested a visit to Len Seager in hospital, but he wasn't sure he could handle it, at least not on his own. I think going with us could be the answer.'

'Why didn't he want to go?'

'I'm not absolutely certain. He said first of all that he didn't like hospitals, then he said he didn't think he could handle seeing Len so badly injured, but I have a feeling there's more to it than that.'

'Maybe we'll find out what it is if he goes to the hospital with us,' said David thoughtfully.

'I've been talking to Louise,' said Rachel, 'and she's going to start making enquiries about Len going to Conway House.'

'Good.' His eyes met hers. 'And what about you—are you still going to raise the subject with your parents about Jennifer going there, or have you changed your mind?'

'Why should I have changed my mind?'

He shrugged but his gaze didn't leave hers and somehow she found it impossible to look away, as, instinctively, she knew he was thinking of the moment in the car the night before when he had touched her hand and she had pulled away so sharply.

'Of course I haven't changed my mind,' she said. 'I shall be seeing them at the weekend.'

He frowned slightly and suddenly she longed to say something, to try and explain why she had acted the way she had. She knew why she had pulled away from him the night before—because she couldn't allow herself to become remotely interested in him. What she couldn't understand was why she felt so bad about it. Helplessly she watched him leave her office.

Rachel's opportunity to speak to her parents came on Saturday morning after the community nurse had arrived and was tending to Jennifer in her room and she and her parents were sitting at the kitchen table. Her mother, who looked extremely tired, had already commented on the fact that she had had yet another sleepless night.

'What exactly is keeping you awake, Mum?' asked

Rachel casually, knowing full well what her mother's reply would be.

'After I get out to see to Jennifer I can't get back to sleep. I used to be able to, but just lately I've found it's impossible; once I'm awake I start worrying about the silliest things.'

'How often do you have to see to Jennifer?'

Her mother shrugged. 'Three, sometimes four times a night. We used to take it in turns, didn't we, Ken?' She glanced at her husband who was reading the morning paper. 'But when I'm already awake I don't have the heart to wake him.' She stood up and walked to the sink.

'I've told you, I don't mind.' Her husband sounded irritable.

Rachel took a deep breath and glanced from one to the other then over her shoulder at the closed door of her sister's ground-floor bedroom. The faint murmur of voices could be heard from inside as Jennifer talked to the nurse.

'Have you thought about any sort of respite care for Jennifer?' She tried to keep her tone light, matter-of-fact, but her mother swung round from the sink where she had just begun to prepare vegetables for lunch, and her father lowered his paper and peered over his glasses at her.

'What do you mean?' Her mother frowned.

'Somewhere that Jennifer could be cared for to give you both a break.'

'I don't want her going into a home,' her father said flatly.

# TAKE 4 LOVE ON CALL ROMANCES FREE

*Mills & Boon Love on Call romances capture all the excitement, intrigue and emotion of a busy medical world. But a world never too busy to ignore love and romance.*

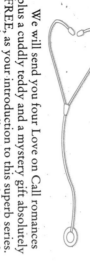

We will send you four Love on Call romances plus a cuddly teddy and a mystery gift absolutely FREE, as your introduction to this superb series.

At the same time we'll reserve a subscription for you to our Reader Service. Every month you could receive the latest four Love on Call romances delivered direct to your door postage and packing FREE, plus our FREE Newsletter packed with author news, competitions, special offers and much more.

What's more, there's no obligation. You may cancel or suspend your subscription at any time. So you've nothing to lose and a whole world of romance to gain!

## YOUR GIFT

Return this card today and we'll send you this lovely cuddly teddy bear absolutely FREE.

*Fill in the Free Books Certificate overleaf* ▼ ▼

# Free Books Certificate

**Yes!** Please send me four FREE Love on Call romances together with my FREE cuddly teddy and mystery gift. Please also reserve a special Reader Service subscription for me. If I decide to subscribe, I shall receive four brand new books every month for just £7.20, postage and packing FREE. If I decide not to subscribe, I shall write to you within 10 days. Any free books and gifts will be mine to keep in any case.
I understand that I am under no obligation whatsoever - I may cancel or suspend my subscription at any time simply by writing to you.
I am over 18 years of age.

## Your Extra Bonus Gift

We all love mysteries, so as well as the books and cuddly teddy we've an intriguing gift just for you. No clues - send off today!

1A4D

Ms/Mrs/Miss/Mr _____

Address _____

_____

Postcode _____ Signature _____

NO STAMP NEEDED

**Mills & Boon
Reader Service
FREEPOST
PO Box 236
Croydon
CR9 9EL**

▲ Send No Money Now

'I didn't exactly mean that. . .'

'When this started, we agreed we would care for her here, and that's what we're going to do.'

'What did you mean, Rachel?' her mother asked slowly, ignoring her husband's indignant look.

'I simply meant somewhere for Jennifer to go on a regular basis for short periods of time simply to give you both a rest. In fact, I'm surprised the community nurse hasn't suggested something on those lines.'

'She did once.' Ken Stevens stood up and folded his newspaper. 'But we told her we weren't interested.'

'I didn't realise there were places quite like that,' said her mother wearily, pushing her hair out of her eyes. 'I imagined if we agreed to Jennifer going somewhere that would be that and she wouldn't come home again.'

'No.' Rachel shook her head. 'It wouldn't be like that at all.' She swallowed, then, taking another deep breath, she said quickly, 'In fact there's a place on the other side of town; it's called Conway House and it caters especially for handicapped people. . .'

'I've heard of that place.' Her father snorted. 'It's for the subnormal; no daughter of mine is going there!'

'Ken, will you please be quiet for a minute and listen to what Rachel has to say?' his wife rounded on him sharply.

'It's for both mentally and physically handicapped people,' explained Rachel. 'Most of the residents are there on a permanent basis, but there's a brand-new wing that has just been opened and is almost exclusively for short-term patients—people like Jennifer who can't be left alone, who need constant attention.'

'Jennifer would hate it,' said Ken Stevens bluntly.

'I thought that at first, Dad,' said Rachel, 'but I've changed my mind. It's a lovely place with excellent facilities. There would be far more activities for Jennifer than we could ever hope to provide for her here.'

'How do you know that? Have you been there?' Her father glared at her as if he suspected her of having the whole thing arranged behind his back.

'Yes, I have, as a matter of fact. David offered to show me the place and. . .'

'David? David who?'

Rachel straightened her shoulders, knowing it had to be said. 'David Markham, Dad.'

'David Markham! What the hell has he got to do with it?'

'He works at Conway House,' explained Rachel.

'I thought he worked at OBEX,' said her mother with a frown.

'He does, but only for part of the week; the rest of the time he works at Conway House.'

'And I suppose it was him who suggested Jennifer going there.'

Rachel could sense her father's anger rising and she knew she had to defuse the situation quickly.

'No, he didn't, as a matter of fact; it was my idea. . .
I thought. . .'

'Well, you can think again,' said her father
angrily. 'I don't know how you can even suggest it.
Why, only a couple of weeks ago you were saying
you hoped they wouldn't even meet at the Family
Day; now you're suggesting that she actually goes
and stays where he works. Don't you think that man
has done enough harm to Jennifer as it is without
inflicting any more pain on her?'

Rachel shrugged helplessly and turned to her
mother.

'Why did you suggest it, Rachel?' Valerie Stevens
was as puzzled as her husband but without his anger.

'I suppose I've seen another side to David
Markham since I've been working with him.'

'Oh, so he's charmed you now as well, has he?'
said her father.

'Of course not. It's just that he seems so caring. . .
in the work he does with the handicapped. . .'

'Caring? Markham?' Her father gave a short
laugh. 'He wouldn't know the meaning of the word.
Come on, Rachel, think about it; a caring man
would hardly have walked out on his future wife as
soon as he learned she had a crippling disease, would
he? You're too gullible, my girl, that's your trouble.'
With that he turned and marched from the kitchen,
leaving Rachel and her mother staring at each other.

'Take no notice of him.' Valerie sighed. 'He's
been very uptight just lately.'

'Exactly. He needs a holiday—you both do—and

I saw this as a way to ensure that you could get regular time off in the future.'

'I know you did, dear, and I appreciate it, I really do, and so will your father when he's had time to think about it; but you must admit, he does have a point—about David Markham, I mean. We could hardly expect Jennifer to want to go to that place if he's going to be there.'

'She would hardly see him. His work is mainly with the permanent residents. He very rarely goes to the Rosemount wing.'

'Even so, I think we'd better let the matter drop, at least for the time being, and let your father calm down.'

'Have you said anything to Jennifer about David being back in the area again?'

'No.' Her mother shook her head. 'I couldn't bring myself to tell her and I'm pretty sure your father won't have said anything.'

'Well, it's Family Day next weekend; don't you think it might be the thing to do to mention it? Then if they do happen to meet it won't come as such a shock to her.'

'Maybe I will. . .I just wish I knew how she will take it,' her mother said anxiously.

'You never know, it may not bother her after all this time. It seems to me that parents carry these things on longer than the people involved—even Irene Markham seemed offhand with me, though God knows what she's got to be huffy about.'

'Irene Markham! When did you see her?' Her mother's eyes widened in amazement.

'I had to go to her house.'

'Whatever for?'

'To pick David up—surprising as it seems, he's apparently living there with her. I should imagine it's only a temporary arrangement until he finds a place of his own. . .'

'But what were you doing picking him up?'

'His car was being serviced and it was the night he was going to show me Conway House.'

The silence in the kitchen was broken only by the whirring of the washing machine as it finished its programme.

'Rachel,' said her mother at last, 'you aren't getting involved with him, are you?'

'Of course I'm not.' She laughed. 'What a suggestion!' She paused, then, catching sight of her mother's dubious expression, she said, 'Honestly, Mum, you don't seriously think I'd get involved with him after Jennifer's experience? And besides, who would want Irene Markham as a mother-in-law?'

They both laughed and her mother said, 'Yes, Irene always was a bit formidable. I take it she hasn't changed?'

'Not in that respect, but I did think she was looking a lot older.'

'Were you there for long?'

'No, only a few minutes. That was quite long enough. As I said, she didn't exactly seem enthralled to see me.'

'What happened when you took him home? Did you have to go in again?'

Rachel shook her head. 'No, David asked me to go back for coffee but I refused.' She hesitated.

'And?' Her mother appeared to be waiting.

'And what?' She found herself playing for time.

'What happened then?'

She took a deep breath. 'We went for a meal instead.'

'Rachel. . .' There was a warning tone in Valerie Stevens' voice which Rachel knew only too well.

'There's no need to sound like that, Mum,' she protested. 'I can assure you, it was only a simple meal in a pub, so don't go reading anything more into it.'

To Rachel's relief the community nurse emerged at that moment from Jennifer's bedroom and the conversation switched from David Markham, and for the rest of the day neither he nor Conway House was mentioned again. Then just as she was preparing to leave to return to her flat her mother invited her to Sunday lunch.

'Oh, I'm sorry, Mum,' she said quickly, 'I won't be able to make it tomorrow.' She was aware of her mother's raised eyebrows and knew she had to give a reason. 'I'm going out with some friends—from work,' she added, then had the uncomfortable feeling that her mother knew exactly whom she was going out with.

Rachel knew, however, there was no point trying to explain that she was merely going with David to see her new friends from Conway House, because it looked as if her mother, together with Nina, Greg and all the others, had jumped to conclusions and were ready to believe that what was a perfectly innocent friendship had developed into something more.

# CHAPTER SEVEN

ON SUNDAY morning Rachel awoke to bright autumn sunshine and clear blue skies. David had told her they would pick her up in the minibus to save her driving her car all the way to the woods. After a leisurely breakfast she showered and dressed in black leggings and a loose cherry-red sweater that was a perfect contrast to her dark hair, then at ten o'clock precisely her doorbell sounded and she locked her flat and ran lightly down the stairs.

David was standing on her doorstep; he was casually dressed in jeans, a navy blue roll-necked sweater and a tan-coloured leather jacket.

Rachel's heart skipped a beat at her first sight of him and if she had been trying to delude herself that David had asked her along purely for the sake of her new friends she was forced to dismiss it as his gaze met hers.

'You look lovely,' he said quietly.

'Thank you.' She was aware that the colour that flooded her cheeks couldn't be blamed on reflection from her sweater. To cover her confusion she looked beyond him into the street. 'Where are you parked?'

'Just down the road. Are you ready? They're making so much noise I think we could be in danger of being moved on for creating a public disturbance.'

'Yes, I'm ready.' She closed the door behind her and joined him on the pavement and as she took several breaths of the crisp October air she suddenly felt how good it was to be alive. Church bells sounded across the city and as they crossed the road they could see two brightly painted barges chugging away up the canal beneath the overhanging willows.

Alf, the Conway House driver, had parked his bus at the end of the road, and, as they approached, Rachel could see the passengers waving to them. Happily she waved back, realising just how pleased she was to see them again and when, moments later, she climbed into the crowded bus with David behind her she was deafened by welcoming voices. Even Sybil seemed pleased to see her and immediately she was pulled down to sit between Danny and Belinda, while David resumed his seat beside the driver.

On the drive to Pelham Woods Rachel realised just how short the concentration span was of some members of the group. Even those who had given her the most rapturous of welcomes soon forgot her, easily distracted by events outside the bus, while games of I-Spy were abandoned almost before they were started.

At the other extreme, Belinda attached herself with limpet-like tenacity, as Rachel remembered she had done previously in the swimming-pool, doggedly refusing to be distracted by any other diversion, engrossed only in Rachel's clothes, her hair and the colour of her lipstick.

Danny had mercifully been persuaded to leave his

ghetto-blaster behind, but this had been against his better judgement, and Rachel soon realised his silence was in fact a form of sulking. She did her best to draw him out of his depression but in so doing roused Belinda's jealousy, as she, in turn, also indulged in a fit of sulks.

'Take no notice,' said Sybil matter-of-factly. 'This sort of thing happens all the time. It'll all be forgotten when we get to the woods, you'll see. They're going to collect conkers for the championships tonight.'

And she was right. From the moment they all tumbled out of the minibus on the edge of the woods, the prime objective was to see who could collect the most conkers.

The trees were rich in autumnal glory, the golds, russets and copper contrasting strongly with the bottle-green of a belt of fir trees etched against the deep blue of the October sky. Rachel and David joined in the quest for the green cases that housed the shiny brown conkers and soon pockets and paper bags were bulging as the collection grew, while the sound of spontaneous laughter hung in the still air.

Later, while Sybil dispensed orange juice in plastic beakers and handed out pink wafers biscuits, David joined Rachel on a moss-covered bank where she had sat down to rest.

'They can be tiring, can't they?' He nodded towards the group who were silent for the moment, their concentration on eating and drinking.

'True, but their joy in everything makes it all

worthwhile. I must admit, though, I find it difficult to keep up with their thought patterns at times.'

He laughed. 'And just when you think you have caught up with them they've moved on to something else.' At that moment Belinda looked over her shoulder and, seeing them together, detached herself from the rest of the group and tramped through the dying bracken towards them.

'Looks as if Belinda has just realised she doesn't have your undivided attention,' he commented, and Rachel gave a rueful smile.

Belinda stopped in front of them, still drinking her orange juice and rocking backwards and forwards on her heels. She was wearing a bright pink tracksuit with a transfer across the front.

'Do you like Michael Jackson, Belinda?' asked Rachel, pointing to the transfer.

She nodded, spilling juice down her front so that it trickled down the pop star's face. 'He's my boyfriend,' she stated.

'Is he, now?' Rachel smiled and searched her memory to ask something about one of his latest records, but before she had the chance to say anything Belinda said, 'Is David your boyfriend?'

'No, Belinda,' Rachel answered quickly, only too aware of the amused expression on David's face. 'David isn't my boyfriend—we just work together.'

'Who is your boyfriend?' Belinda wiped her mouth with the back of her hand.

'I don't have one.'

Belinda stopped drinking and stared at her. 'You must have one.'

'Well, I had one once.' Rachel laughed, almost apologetically.

'What was his name?'

She hesitated, but the mulish expression on Belinda's face indicated that she wasn't about to be fobbed off. 'Ian,' she admitted at last.

'Ian what?'

'Ian White.' She glanced at David and wryly saw that he seemed to be listening to this conversation with great interest. Then to her amusement Belinda turned her attention to him.

'Who's your girlfriend?'

'I don't have a girlfriend, Belinda.'

'Did you have one once too?' Her gaze was solemn, unblinking.

'Yes, I had one once. Her name was Jennifer,' he added.

Rachel stiffened, wondering what was coming next, thinking that Belinda might ask why Jennifer wasn't his girlfriend any longer and wondering how he would answer, but she hadn't bargained for Belinda's line of reasoning.

'Rachel will be your girlfriend,' she said simply. 'Won't you, Rachel? She's my friend as well, but I don't mind.'

'Thank you, Belinda,' said David seriously.

Affectionately they watched her as she ambled back to the others, kicking fallen leaves in front of her as she went.

'Well, that's settled, then,' he said with a grin. 'From now on you're officially my girlfriend.'

Rachel didn't reply, wondering suddenly, wildly, just what that would feel like — to be his girlfriend.

He half turned to look at her. 'Who was Ian White?' The question was casual but somehow inevitable.

'A junior registrar at St Clare's,' she said, then, seeing his blank look, explained, 'He came after you left.'

'So what happened?'

'What do you mean?' She shifted slightly on the moss and felt the damp seep through her leggings.

'You said he was your boyfriend once; now he isn't, and I just wondered why.'

She shrugged. 'It didn't work out, that's all.'

'How long were you together?'

'About a year.' Suddenly she was surprised that she could talk about Ian White without regret; surprised to find that it didn't hurt any more.

'What went wrong?' David's voice was low, gentle, in no way as if he was prying, but rather from concern.

She hesitated, then with the point of her shoe touched a clump of fungi that grew round the roots of a large oak tree, drawing back as one burst open. 'He was very possessive,' she said at last. 'He wanted me to spend every spare minute with him.'

'I can't say I blame him for that.'

She looked at him, their eyes met and quickly she looked away again. There was something in his expression she wasn't sure she could cope with. 'You don't understand,' she said at last. 'I don't have a lot of spare time.'

'But if he was a registrar he must surely have understood that you had to work shifts.'

'It wasn't that, it was the amount of time I have to spend at home. . .helping with Jennifer,' she added.

There was a long pause then Rachel went on, 'Ian wasn't prepared to put up with that, and I decided if his understanding wouldn't stretch that far I was better off without him.'

In the silence that followed she wondered what David was thinking, then, at a sudden shout from Danny, they both looked up. He was beckoning to them and they could see that the group was preparing to move off.

Rachel stood up, brushing twigs and leaves from her clothes, then she turned to David who was still sitting on the bank staring up at her.

'Are you coming?' she asked, and when he still made no attempt to get up she said, 'What is it, why are you staring at me?'

Without a word, he stood up, then, moving towards her, he stretched out his hand towards her hair. She stood motionless, wondering what he was about to do, and as he moved closer she suddenly had the ridiculous impression he was going to kiss her.

Every nerve in her body was taut, stretched to breaking-point; gently he took something from her hair, holding up a small twig for her to see.

Then softly, his eyes never leaving hers, he said, 'I think we'd better join the others.'

They completed a circular walk through the woods, tramping through leaves and bracken and ending up back at the minibus where Sybil announced it was time to go back to Conway House for lunch.

Rachel was invited to join them and she was happy to do so, but for the rest of the day she couldn't forget that moment when David had moved so close to her; she couldn't forget the look in his eyes, a look that had implied that the conclusions drawn by others about his intentions towards her could be well founded.

And later that afternoon when he drove her home in his car and he seemed unusually quiet, she sensed that he too was remembering that moment.

He brought the car to a halt outside her flat and they sat motionless, staring at a group of boys who were playing on skateboards.

'Are you going to ask me in?' he asked at last.

'I'm not sure that I should.'

'I think there's every reason that you should; after all, according to Belinda you're my girlfriend now.' He smiled then, lightening the tension that had grown between them.

'All right——' she too smiled '——come and have a cup of tea.'

He followed her up the stairs to her flat and as she let them in he said, 'If only real life were as uncomplicated as Belinda's world.'

'You implied to Belinda that there hadn't been anyone in your life since Jennifer,' said Rachel as she led him into her kitchen.

'Is that so unbelievable?' He walked across to the window.

'Maybe not unbelievable, but surprising. I imagined there might have been someone in Australia.'

'I dated other women, certainly, but there wasn't anyone serious.' He leaned forward as he spoke, looking out across the city, past the canal to the cathedral beyond. 'What a fantastic view you have from here.'

'Yes, it's wonderful,' she agreed, filling the kettle. Then, steering the conversation back on course, she said, 'Are you saying it took you a long time to get over Jennifer?'

'What do you think? We were engaged, after all.'

She frowned as she began taking mugs from the cupboard. 'I know, but. . .'

'Rachel, I don't want to talk about Jennifer. I know she's your sister and I'm desperately sorry about what's happened to her. I loved her very much once, but it's over now, it's in the past.'

Suddenly she was aware that he had moved in closely behind her and before she even had time to think his arms went round her. She tensed, preparing to struggle, but purposefully he turned her to face him and before she had chance to utter one single protest he cupped her face in his strong hands and brought his lips down on hers, silencing anything she might have been about to say.

Wildly Rachel's mind raced ahead. What was he doing? This was sheer madness. Nothing could ever come of it.

Then gradually she became aware of the demanding nature of his kiss and her own desire flared to match his. In sudden abandon she allowed her arms to creep up round his neck, her fingers to sink into the short hair at the back of his head while at the same time parting her lips and welcoming the exciting exploration of his tongue.

It was only when his embrace became more adventurous, his hands more demanding as he became aroused, that she realised where they were heading and she finally found the strength to pull away from him.

'This is lunacy,' she gasped. 'Please, David, stop it.'

'But why. . .?'

'It just wouldn't work. . .'

'I don't see why not. It's perfectly obvious we're attracted to each other.'

'Maybe we are, but I can't let myself become involved with you.'

'Why?'

'Oh, David! For God's sake! How can you even ask why?' she cried in exasperation.

His eyes narrowed. 'You mean because of Jennifer?'

'Of course because of Jennifer.'

'I told you, that was over a long time ago.'

'I know it was. But what do you think my parents

would think if I were to become involved with you? How could I ever explain to them and how could I tell Jennifer? How could she ever understand, the way she is now?'

For a long moment he stared at her, then he stepped back, his arms dropping to his sides. 'Rachel, I'm sorry for what's happened to Jennifer, I told you that, but don't you think there's the chance she might just understand?'

'How could she? Why should she? How do you think she would feel seeing us together after what's happened to her?'

'I still think you may be underestimating her.'

'I don't want to risk finding out.'

'So you're saying that to prevent the risk of your sister possibly being hurt at seeing us together you're not prepared to have any sort of relationship with me?' He stepped further away from her and she was shocked at the sudden, inexplicable sense of loss she felt.

'Yes, David, that's right,' she forced herself to say. 'I'm sorry, but that's the way it has to be.'

'And are you prepared to go on living the rest of your life in tune to your sister's wishes?'

'What do you mean?' She stared at him.

'You've already admitted that was the cause of your break-up with Ian White. You could end up very lonely at this rate, Rachel, and all for Jennifer's sake.'

'She's worth it,' she retorted.

He was silent for a moment then, softly, he said, 'Are you sure of that?'

She stared at him, wondering if she'd heard right, then something seemed to snap inside her. 'How can you say that?' she cried. 'You, who professed to love her once. Honestly, David, I've doubted in the past that you knew the meaning of the word — now I'm sure of it!'

They glared at each other angrily, then Rachel said, 'I think you'd better go.'

'Yes, I think I had,' he replied tightly. 'Before we say things we might regret.' He turned just as the kettle began to boil, and, the tea forgotten, he strode from the kitchen and out of the flat.

As she heard her front door click, Rachel's anger suddenly turned to dismay and as she turned to the window she found she could only see the outline of the cathedral through a mist of tears.

# CHAPTER EIGHT

FAMILY DAY at OBEX was the highlight of the year, and preparations went on for several weeks in advance. Attractions included a travelling funfair that set up every year on the field beside the factory's private runway and a gigantic firework display during the evening.

Apart from her anxiety over Jennifer's meeting David again, Rachel had been looking forward to Family Day, but when she arrived for work the next morning the preparations were the furthest thing from her mind. She had spent a sleepless night agonising over what had happened between herself and David and she found herself dreading what the atmosphere would be like between them.

Some time in the darkest hours of the night she had been forced to admit to herself that she was deeply attracted to David Markham, just as she now knew he was to her, but recognising that didn't alter the fact that the situation was impossible. His kiss had thrilled and excited her, and the brief time she had spent in his arms had only increased her desire, leaving her aching to know him better.

She had shuddered at the thought of trying to explain her feelings to her parents and her sister, but then David's heartless implication that Jennifer wasn't worth her concern had shocked her beyond measure. If he could behave like that towards a woman he had once loved, a woman rendered helpless, what could she herself expect in the future?

When he arrived that morning David appeared cool towards her — so cool, in contrast to the friendly relationship they had previously established, that Nina noticed it and mentioned it while she and Rachel were working out a list of appointments for management medicals.

'I thought you two had agreed to settle your differences,' she commented after David came into the office for some records, then left without saying a word.

'We did,' said Rachel shortly.

'Oh, come on, Rachel, it's perfectly obvious you've had words,' said Nina, and when Rachel remained silent she went on, 'Just as it's perfectly obvious that you're mad about each other. No, don't keep denying it —' she held up her hand in protest as Rachel opened her mouth '— it just won't wash any more. Everyone knows! Honestly, Rachel, you've only got to see the two of you together — you're just made for each other.'

'Oh, God!' Rachel ran her fingers through her hair. 'If only it were that simple.'

'You mean because of your sister?' asked Nina curiously.

Rachel nodded.

'Is that what this silent treatment is all about this morning?'

'Yes.' She hesitated, uncertain how to go on.

'So what exactly is the problem?' Nina frowned.

Rachel gave a deep sigh. 'I just can't imagine telling them at home. How do you think they would react if I suddenly announced that the new man in my life is the man who ditched my sister five years ago?'

'Well, I can appreciate they're not exactly going to be over the moon, but this is your life we're talking about, not theirs.'

'Even so. . .'

'Rachel, listen to me. What you have to ask yourself is, just how important is David to you?' Nina looked searchingly at her, then nodded. 'As I thought, you don't even have to answer. I can see by the look on your face—he's becoming very important, isn't he?'

Rachel nodded miserably. 'But that doesn't make it any easier. . .'

'I think you may be surprised. Five years is a long time; people change.'

'My parents haven't changed. . .they don't even like the sound of his name.'

'What about your sister?'

'I don't know. I haven't heard her mention David.'

'Well, there you are; after all, she's the one who was most involved, not your parents, and you may find she feels quite differently now.'

'David more or less said the same, but I really don't know what to think. She doesn't even know yet that he's back on the scene, let alone that he's working with me, and as for anything else. . .' She trailed off uncertainly.

'Don't you think it's high time she was told?'

'Yes, but I think my mother is going to do that before Family Day; that's when it could all happen, Nina. I usually look forward to Family Day, but I can honestly say that this year I'm beginning to dread it,' said Rachel, then, picking up a pile of records, she said, 'This won't do, we must get on, otherwise we'll never finish these medicals.'

They worked steadily for the rest of the morning on the management medicals, Rachel and Nina checking weight, testing urine for any signs of sugar diabetes, taking blood samples to test haemoglobin, thyroid function, liver function and cholesterol levels and checking blood-pressure for hypertension. The employees then went on to David, who tested heart and lungs and talked to each of them to ascertain whether there were any personal anxieties that might affect their role in management.

When Rachel was finally writing up her reports at the end of the morning, Nina suddenly called her and asked if she could come and look at a young man who had come in with a skin rash.

'I don't like the look of it,' said Nina. 'His skin is quite blistered.'

Moments later Rachel saw for herself that the man's hands were indeed covered in tiny red blisters.

'Have you been using anything different from usual?' she asked.

He shook his head. 'No, Sister, I don't think so.'

'No new chemicals or anything like that?'

'No. . .'

'We'd better let the doctor have a look; he'll probably prescribe a cream to help clear it up. Wait there a moment, I'll go and ask him.'

David was in his room washing his hands, having just finished the last of the medicals, and he turned from the sink as Rachel knocked and entered.

'Could you see a patient, please?' she asked quietly, avoiding his gaze.

'Of course. What's the problem?'

'A skin rash. Extensive blistering. Shall I ask him to come in?'

'Is he in your room?'

'Yes.'

'I'll come and see him.'

The politeness between them was so precise, so finely tuned, it was almost tangible. As he followed her from the room, he said, 'Has he been using any new chemicals?'

'Apparently not.'

'I see.' He paused. 'Rachel?'

She froze. 'Yes?'

'I was wondering. . .'

'Yes?'

He cleared his throat and she waited, holding her breath and wondering what he was going to say next. 'I was wondering if you still wanted to go and see Len Seager?'

She breathed out. How could she have imagined

he was going to say anything else? 'Of course, why shouldn't I?'

He shrugged. 'I just wondered, that's all. When would you like to go?'

'I don't mind. Tonight? Tomorrow night?'

'Tonight would be fine. I'll see Jimmy Warren and make sure he still wants to come with us.' By this time they had reached the office and as David caught sight of the man sitting beside Rachel's desk he said, 'Is this the patient?'

Rachel nodded. 'Yes, this is Bob Lane.'

David carefully examined the man's hands. 'It certainly looks like some sort of allergy or chemical reaction,' he said.

'Could it be the new adhesive we've been using?' asked the man suddenly.

'A new adhesive? Yes, it could well be that.' David glanced at Rachel and she sighed.

'You told me you hadn't been using any different chemicals, Bob.'

'Well, I never gave the adhesive a thought,' Bob Lane said slowly. 'Although now I come to think about it, I had my doubts from the start.'

'Why's that?' asked David.

'It were the smell. Dreadful. I know the smell of our usual adhesive isn't exactly pleasant, but this one's diabolical.'

'You wear gloves, of course?'

The man looked uncomfortable. 'Well, Doc, I do normally but I didn't over the weekend.'

'You were on the weekend shift?'

'Yes.' He moved uneasily on his chair. 'I needed new gloves and I thought I'd wait until Monday when they're normally issued.'

'You could have got them, though?' asked Rachel quickly.

'Oh, yes, I just didn't want to bother anyone.'

David began writing on a prescription pad. 'I'll give you some cortisone cream and I want you to wear cotton gloves for a few days, then come back and see me. Before you go, Sister Clarey will give you a Vitalograph to test your lungs to make sure you haven't inhaled any harmful vapours from this stuff.'

After Bob Lane had gone David turned to Rachel and shook his head in mild exasperation.

'I'd better do a report on that adhesive,' she said. 'It could be that it's just something that Bob is allergic to, but it had better be investigated and some sample testing done in case we need to get on to the manufacturers. We don't want any accusations of negligence.'

'No, one of those at a time is quite enough,' replied David grimly.

Rachel frowned. 'What do you mean?'

'Apparently Len Seager is trying to sue the company through his union for negligence.'

'Do you think he has a case?'

'I don't know. The union is meeting this afternoon to discuss the results of tests taken on Len at the time of the accident. I shall see the representative later and he should be able to tell me whether Len has a case or not. The tests could prove all-conclusive, especially as there was only one witness to the accident.'

'Yes,' she nodded. 'And that a witness who seems reluctant even to go and see the patient, let alone state what he saw or get involved in a compensation claim.'

David shrugged and strode out of her room. Miserably she picked up her pen to write her report, thinking that, before, he would have stayed and chatted to her.

Jimmy Warren's reluctance was still very much in evidence that evening when Rachel met him and David in the foyer of the big county hospital on the far side of the city. David hadn't been on duty at the factory that afternoon and Rachel had wondered if he would suggest picking her up from her flat and taking her to the hospital, but he hadn't, and his failure to do so only emphasised the coolness that was rapidly growing between them.

Jimmy, dressed in jeans and a black leather jacket, had arrived on his motorbike. He seemed edgy and ill at ease and as they took the lift up to the fourth floor and stepped out into the corridor his eyes darted from side to side as if he was terrified at what he might be about to see.

'Don't worry, Jimmy.' Rachel tried to reassure him. 'It won't be so bad and I'm sure Len will be pleased to see you.'

When David explained to the ward sister who they

were, she escorted them to Len's bed. He was lying flat, his neck supported by a brace, but his eyes brightened when he saw Rachel.

'Hello, Sister.' He managed a smile. 'Good of you to come.' Then his eyes moved to David. 'And you, Doc,' he added.

'How are you feeling, Len?' asked Rachel inadequately, her heart going out to him in his helplessness.

'Not feeling very much at all just at the moment, Sister,' he joked.

'We've brought someone to see you.' Rachel turned and Jimmy moved forward into Len's line of vision.

'Hello, mate,' Jimmy said, his eyes fixed on Len's face as if he was scared to look at the outline of the rest of his body, lying motionless beneath the sheets.

'Well, I'll be blowed—Jimmy, me lad! It's good to see you.' Len's eyes suddenly filled with tears.

Jimmy gulped and sat down on a chair beside the bed almost as if he didn't trust his legs to support him. 'I brought you these,' he mumbled and thrust a brown paper bag on to the bed.

'That's nice of you.' Len tried to look down. 'What are they?'

'Grapes. . .I thought. . .'

'Thanks, I like grapes. Put them up on the locker, will you? One of the nurses will feed them to me later. It's not all bad in here, you know,' Len went on, catching sight of Jimmy's expression as the full extent of his limitations became apparent to the younger man. 'Mind you, I can't wait to get out.' Silence followed his words and he looked from one to the other of them. 'Oh, I am going to get out,' he said, 'make no mistake about that. They'll fix me up, you'll see. I'll be as right as rain again soon. Just you make sure they get that jig fixed before I come back, Jimmy, me lad; I don't want no repeat performance.'

It was David who broke the silence that followed. 'Actually, Len, that's one of the reasons why I'm here — to talk about where you're going when you get out of here.'

Len blinked rapidly. 'When I get out? I'm going home, of course; where else would I go?'

'You're going to need a lot of looking after, Len,' said David quietly.

Len was silent for a moment then he gave a huge sigh and when he spoke again there was a note of hopelessness in his voice and no sign of the bravado he had shown only moments earlier. 'Yes, Doc, I guess you're right. I won't be going back on no jigs, will I?'

'No, Len,' said David truthfully. 'You won't.'

'Ah, well, there you go. Still, I should be coming in for a tidy sum of compensation. I've asked the union to take up the case for me.' His gaze flickered to Jimmy then back to David again.

'That's the other thing I wanted to talk to you about,' said David.

Rachel glanced at him quickly. There hadn't been time on the way up to ask him what the results of the tests had been or what the union had consequently decided.

'Well, go on, Doc,' said Len, a note of optimism in his voice now. 'How much do you think I'll get?'

'Len, this is all pretty confidential. . .' David began.

'Yes, would you like us to go?' asked Rachel while Jimmy sprang to his feet as if he couldn't wait to get out of the ward.

Len, however, had his gaze fixed on David's face and almost as if he could read his mind, and ignoring the other two, he said roughly, 'They're not taking the case, are they, Doc?'

'No, Len, I'm afraid they aren't. . .I think you know why.'

Len moved his eyes so that he was staring at Jimmy. 'You been talking?'

Jimmy shook his head vigorously. 'No, Len, I haven't, I swear it. I never said a word, did I?' He looked pleadingly at Rachel.

'No, Len, he didn't,' Rachel intervened. 'Jimmy hasn't said anything.'

'Then why won't they. . .?'

It was David who answered, finishing Len's question. 'Take the case? Because of the results of blood tests taken at the time of your accident, Len.'

Len didn't answer, then a sound that could have been a sigh or which might have been a sob escaped his lips, a sound full of despair.

'So,' he said at last, 'I can't move, I can't work, I

can't look after myself, and I haven't got any money. . .what the bloody hell am I going to do?'

'That, Len, is the other thing I want to talk to you about,' said David, drawing up a chair.

'I think Jimmy and I will go and get ourselves a cup of tea and leave you to talk to Len,' said Rachel.

As they turned to go, she heard David say, 'Have you heard of Conway House, Len?'

Ten minutes later Rachel sat opposite Jimmy in the hospital self-service bar as they sipped hot tea from plastic cups.

'What is Conway House?' asked Jimmy curiously.

'It's a residential care centre for handicapped people,' replied Rachel.

Jimmy gave a deep sigh and slumped back in his chair. 'I suppose that's what the doc's suggesting to Len?'

She nodded. 'Yes, Jimmy. But it isn't so bad as it sounds, really it isn't. I've been there and the facilities are marvellous. . .'

'But how is Len going to afford anything like that if he don't get no compensation?' Angrily Jimmy pushed his half-empty cup aside.

'Conway House is run by a charity,' explained Rachel. 'Len will be assessed, and if he qualifies his expenses will be paid.'

Jimmy looked up sharply. 'If he qualifies. . .?'

'He will; you needn't have any doubts about that.'

They were silent for a moment, both apparently deep in their own thoughts, then Rachel looked

across at Jimmy. 'You knew Len was going to try to
sue the company, didn't you?'

He stared at her for a moment then he shrugged
and nodded. 'Yes, I knew. All sorts of people have
been questioning me—the health and safety lot, the
union, management—you name it, they've been to
see me.'

'Well, you were the only witness, Jimmy.'

'You can say that again,' he said grimly.

'You also knew about Len's problem, didn't you?'

He hesitated and Rachel went on quickly, 'It's all
right, Jimmy, we knew as well. . .'

'You mean Management knew?'

'Of course, although no one quite knew what
happened that morning—you were the only one who
knew that. . .that is, until the results of the blood
tests were made available.'

'I suppose they showed he'd been drinking?'

'Apparently so and if that's proved then Len
wouldn't have a hope in hell of bringing a case.'

'I didn't want to be the one to pull the rug out,'
said Jimmy. 'Len and I have always been good
mates. Oh, I knew he was drinking, drinking heavily
at that, but there wasn't much I could do about it.
He was usually OK when he came to work.'

'Except for the morning of the accident?'

'Yeah, except for that morning,' agreed Jimmy. 'I
could tell he'd been drinking as soon as he joined
me on the jig. He was very unsteady on his feet. I
kept hoping the foreman would notice, but he didn't;
there was some meeting going on and he seemed

more concerned with the fact that all the bosses were going to that than in what we were doing.'

'You didn't feel inclined to report him?'

Jimmy shook his head. 'You don't grass on a mate,' he said, and fell silent.

'How are the nightmares?' asked Rachel after a while, and he glanced up quickly then looked away again.

'About the same—I still keep seeing his face when he fell.'

'Maybe they will get less now,' said Rachel gently, then, looking up, she said, 'Here comes Dr Markham.'

David sat down beside them and Rachel said anxiously, 'How did Len take the idea of Conway House?'

'He wasn't too enthralled at first but he listened after a while and I've left him thinking about it. He asked if you'd gone, Jimmy. I said if you hadn't I'd get you to go back for a chat with him.'

'I think that's a very good idea, Jimmy,' said Rachel, seeing the expression that crossed his face. Before he had time to refuse, she added, 'As I said to you before, I think you and Len both need to talk over what happened that day. It should be a lot easier now that everything's out in the open and it should help you to come to terms with things, as well as Len.'

He still looked a bit dubious and David said, 'One thing you can tell Len, something I forgot, was that I made enquiries today about his parrot and it appears that if he does go to Conway House he'll be able to take the parrot with him. Tell him that, Jimmy; it just might help to cheer him up.'

They watched in silence as Jimmy made his way to the door; as he disappeared from their view, Rachel sighed.

'It's hard to help people accept that their lives have changed beyond recognition.'

David nodded. 'The hardest part is getting people who have previously been fit, healthy and independent to realise that they need help and support.'

'That's fine when the help and support is there,' said Rachel coolly, then, allowing her eyes to meet his, she said, 'It's when that support is withdrawn that the real tragedy occurs.'

Then she stood up and without a backward glance she walked from the cafeteria.

## CHAPTER NINE

To RACHEL'S growing misery the strained air of politeness continued between herself and David throughout the rest of the week, then on Friday morning, the day before Family Day, he sought her out in her office.

'I was wondering if you intended going swimming later today?' he asked.

'I hadn't, why?' She tried to avoid his gaze but found it impossible.

'I'm bringing the group over from Conway House and I promised Belinda I would ask you.'

She hesitated, wanting to go but feeling she should refuse.

'Belinda will be very disappointed if you aren't there,' he said.

'All right, I'll be there.' She smiled faintly and her breath caught in her throat at his answering expression. Quickly she looked away, fiddling with papers on her desk, not sure she could cope with the anguish in his eyes that mirrored her own, but David lingered.

'Rachel, I've been wanting to ask you, did you ask Jennifer about going to Conway House?'

She shook her head. 'No, David, I haven't actually asked Jennifer yet.'

'But you intend doing so?'

'I'm not certain. I. . .I broached the matter with my parents. . .'

'And?' He raised his eyebrows and waited for her to continue.

'They weren't exactly enthralled with the idea.'

'That's not an unusual reaction; in fact it's what I would expect. I imagine they're still adamant that they want to care for Jennifer themselves. And that's quite understandable.'

'It'll destroy them if they don't ease up soon,' said Rachel flatly. 'My mother especially is becoming worn out with the constant caring and the sleepless nights.'

'And yet she wasn't interested in any respite care?'

'I think she might have been with a bit of persuasion; it was my father who was against it. And then. . .' She paused. 'I'm sorry, David, but when they knew you were at Conway House, that decided the matter.'

'I'm not sure why.' He frowned.

'I suppose they think it would upset Jennifer, your being there.'

'I can't see why.'

'I would have thought it was pretty obvious. . .'

'Not to me it isn't. And while we're on the subject, Rachel, what did you mean the other night when you said the real tragedy for anyone facing up to a handicap was when expected support was withdrawn?'

She stared at him in bewilderment. 'Surely I don't

have to spell it out. . .? Honestly, David, if you don't know what you did to Jennifer. . .'

His eyes narrowed and he was on the verge of saying more when Nina put her head round the door.

'Oh, sorry.' She looked from one to the other. 'Am I interrupting something?'

'No, it's all right, Nina,' said Rachel, still looking at David. 'What did you want?'

'I want David to look at another skin rash. It's that same adhesive — it looks as if it will have to be withdrawn; there's definitely some harmful irritant in it.'

'All right, Nina, I'm just coming.' He watched as Nina disappeared then he turned back to Rachel. There was a strange expression on his face, one she hadn't seen before, and a little shiver touched her spine. 'We'll continue this discussion another time,' he said quietly, 'somewhere we won't be disturbed. I think there are one or two things that need straightening out.'

He strode from her office, leaving Rachel wondering what on earth he could mean. As far as she was concerned things were perfectly straight. He and Jennifer had been engaged to be married, then when she had been diagnosed as having multiple sclerosis he had left her and gone to Australia to work. What could be more straightforward than that?

She didn't see David again until late afternoon when her shift was over and she joined the group from Conway House in the swimming-pool. She had brought herself a new swimsuit but after she had changed she'd stared critically at herself in the mirror in the changing-room. Green eyes stared back at her from beneath dark slanting brows but with her short hair that accentuated her elfin face she somehow felt the swimsuit only made her slight figure look even more boyish.

When she stepped from the changing-room and walked to the poolside, however, she was greeted with the usual enthusiasm, especially from Belinda, who attached herself once again and trailed round the pool behind her, loudly voicing her admiration, and, to Rachel's embarrassment, drawing attention to the new swimsuit.

'It's nice, isn't it, David?' Belinda turned as David appeared. 'Nice colour, pink. I like pink, don't you? Rachel looks nice, doesn't she?'

'Yes, Belinda, Rachel looks very nice,' agreed David, stepping back, and, to her confusion, eyeing her up and down. 'But then. . .' he paused and she wondered what he was going to say '. . .she always looks nice.'

'Y-e-s. . .' admitted Belinda, obviously giving the matter great thought '. . .but I like that pink.' She looked down at her own blue and orange striped suit. 'It's nicer than mine. I wish I had a pink one.' She fell into step between David and Rachel and as they walked around the poolside she looked from one to the other. They stopped when they reached Sybil, who was already in the water, and Belinda put her hands on her hips. 'David's Rachel's boyfriend,' she announced.

'Is he, now?' Sybil said in amusement.

Rachel, who had already been battling with unpredictable sensations brought on by the close proximity of David clad only in his brief black swimming-trunks, felt her cheeks flame and couldn't bring herself to look at him. Then Sybil held up her hand to help Belinda down the steps into the water.

Belinda hovered on the steps, however, testing the water with her toes. 'Ooh, it's cold. . .' she protested.

'You say that every week,' said Sybil with a laugh. 'Come on in, quickly, that's right; cover your shoulders and you'll soon feel warm.'

Rachel followed a squealing Belinda down the steps while David walked up to the deep end, dived in and swam back to join the rest of the group.

Soon they were all engaged in a noisy, boisterous game of hand-ball and, although Rachel joined in as enthusiastically as anyone, as the game progressed she was only really conscious of the mounting awareness between herself and David.

Wherever she looked he was watching her, when she turned to throw the ball he was beside her, his lean, tanned body glistening with thousands of drops of water accidentally brushing against hers, his touch like sudden little electric shocks, both unexpected and thrilling as the game became like some tantalising water charade.

Then, just when Rachel was feeling she wanted it

to go on forever, this exciting masquerade between the two of them where it seemed as if the rest of the world didn't exist, she found herself beside Danny who began stuttering and waving his arms, obviously trying to tell her something.

'What is it, Danny?' she asked, flicking the water from her eyes and smoothing back her hair, only too aware as she did so of David's eyes on her, admiring her figure, her small, high breasts, her long, coltish limbs.

'Out there. . .' Danny shouted excitedly, pointing to the high windows that surrounded the pool.

'What's out there?' Out of the corner of her eye she saw that David had dived below the surface.

'A fair. . .there's a fair. I want to go. I want to go to the fair.'

David surfaced beside them, his thigh brushing hers. 'We'll see if we can get you there, Danny,' he said.

'Now?' asked Danny.

'No, not now, Danny. Tomorrow,' said David patiently, while Rachel felt her heart lurch. That meant David was definitely intending to be at the Family Day. She had still been half hoping that he might not be going to attend, especially as Family Day was on a Saturday when he wasn't officially on duty.

'I want to go now,' shouted Danny at the top of his voice.

'It's no good now, old man,' said David; 'the fair isn't open yet; they're still setting it up.'

But Danny was beyond reasoning with and he had to be taken from the pool kicking and shouting. It heralded the end of the session, as Danny's mood seemed to transmit itself to the others and they too became restless.

At a signal from Sybil, Rachel helped to coax them out of the water and into the changing-rooms where David was helping Danny to dress.

When the group were all finally back in their minibus Rachel and David went through the now expected ritual of waving them goodbye.

'Danny will be going on about the fair all night now,' said David as the bus disappeared through the factory gates, then as they turned away he asked, 'Are you on duty tomorrow?'

She hesitated before answering, still apprehensive about what the next day would bring. 'Not officially. The company always bring St John's Ambulance Brigade in for Family Day.'

'But you will be there?'

'Yes, David, I will be there,' she replied and allowed her gaze to meet his.

'Good,' he said softly. 'It wouldn't be the same without you.'

For a long moment they stared at each other and it was as if the body language they had shared in the pool had ceased to be a game and the strained politeness of the last week had never been. In that instant all she wanted was for him to take her in his arms again; to know the sweet pressure of his mouth

on hers and to feel once more the way her body had
come alive beneath his hands.

It was as if they were the only two people on
earth; oblivious to the crowds who poured from the
factory entrances as the day shift ended and who
milled around them, they had eyes only for each
other. Of the fact that they attracted amused glances
and speculative nudges, they were totally unaware
as they read and interpreted the message in each
other's eyes.

Rachel drove to her flat unknowing and surprisingly
uncaring of what was happening, only conscious of
her desire for David, which somehow, like Danny's
needs, had suddenly erupted and was in urgent need
of fulfilment.

She had time only to park her car and let herself
into her flat before he arrived.

She heard his footsteps on the stairs and was only
aware of the thrill that coursed through her. Everything else was forgotten: Jennifer, Ian White, the
past, everything; the only aspect of any importance
was their overwhelming need for each other.

That questions and recriminations would creep in
later she had little doubt, but for the moment she
simply wanted to shut out the rest of the world, to
step back into that circle of magic they had created,
first in the pool, then in the factory car park when
they had somehow made the rest of the world
go away.

The next moment she was in his arms and he had kicked the door shut behind him.

'Rachel, I'm sorry,' he groaned, lifting her face to his and gazing searchingly into her eyes, 'I can't go on pretending any longer.'

'David.' There was only time to whisper his name before his lips claimed hers in a kiss of such tenderness and passion that her doubts were scattered along with any inhibitions she might have been harbouring.

Moments later, their clothes in a trail that echoed their urgency, they lay in each other's arms on Rachel's bed. To her it felt right to be there with David, her skin soft against his, her senses alive to his touch, and she succeeded in banishing her fears of what would happen when they stepped out of their circle of magic and back into the real world.

He was a restrained and sophisticated lover and, once his initial surge of passion was quieted, his concentration was focused on giving her more pleasure than it was possible to imagine. For Rachel, who had never before experienced such intensity of feeling, it was as if he'd transported her to another world—a world where every sensation was heightened, every touch the prelude to yet more delight as he explored and worshipped every inch of her body before taking her to the peak of fulfilment.

Afterwards she clung to him, the tears wet on her cheeks, and for a long time they lay together in silence as the light of the October evening faded around them.

In the end it was David who spoke first, drawing her even closer to him and pulling the duvet round them both. 'Has that dispelled your doubts?' he murmured.

'What do you mean?' Her reply was drowsy, her thoughts unfocused.

'The doubts you had about my intentions?'

'I never had any doubts about your intentions.' She gave a laugh and he pressed himself closer to her beneath the cover.

'All right, then, the doubts you had about your feelings.'

'You mean my feelings towards you?'

'If you like.'

'I don't think I really had any doubts about them,' she said slowly at last.

'You mean you wanted me from the moment you saw me?' He chuckled and she gave him a light punch on the shoulder.

Then, growing serious, she sighed. 'Oh, David, it wasn't that, you know that. It wasn't anything to do with the way I felt or, for that matter, the way you felt. . .it was. . .'

'I know, in spite of the fact that we agreed not to discuss it, it was all because of what had happened in the past, wasn't it?' When she nodded, he went on, 'It would probably have been better if we had discussed it right at the beginning, and certainly when we realised we were becoming attracted to each other.'

'I simply couldn't imagine telling either Jennifer

or my parents that I was seeing you. . .in fact, I still can't.' She moved restlessly beneath the cover. 'But I can imagine only too well what their reaction will be.'

'They will have to be told, Rachel,' he said gently.

'I know. It's just that I don't want Jennifer, especially, to be hurt any more; she really has had enough.'

'Her illness has been a terrible blow to her, I know, but. . .'

'It wasn't her illness I was referring to, David. That in itself is traumatic enough but——' she swallowed '—it was losing you that really broke her heart. Just think how she's going to feel now when she knows that her own sister is having a relationship with the man who left her.'

In the silence that followed she gradually became aware of David's stillness; so aware that in the end she was forced to twist her head so that she could see his face. His expression was strangely shuttered, however, giving away nothing of the thoughts behind those grey eyes and the low, brooding brows.

'David?' The question, light, whispered, had barely left her lips and seemed to tremble in the air between them, when with a swift unexpected movement, just as she lifted her hand to touch his face, he caught her wrist.

'What is it?' She gave a little gasp as his grip tightened.

'What did you say?' His voice was taut, almost dangerous.

A shiver rippled the length of her spine. 'When?'

'Just now, about Jennifer being hurt.'

'I said her illness had been traumatic enough without. . .'

'Yes, I know, after that.' Sudden impatience flared in his eyes.

She stared, bewildered by his sudden change of mood. 'I said I wondered how she would feel when she knows her own sister is having a relationship with the man who left her. . .David! You're hurting me.' She pulled away from him, rubbing the mark he had left on her wrist.

He continued staring at her, apparently oblivious to the fact that he had hurt her.

'I thought that was what you said,' he muttered, then, drawing in his breath, he put his head back against the pillows and stared at the ceiling.

Puzzled, she watched him. 'David, what is it? What's wrong? I don't understand.'

At last he looked at her. 'Tell me, Rachel——' his tone was even, measured, with no trace of the tender passion of only moments earlier '—why do you think I went to Australia?'

'Well, I. . .that is we. . .what could we think?' She pulled away from him. 'I suppose I assumed you couldn't cope with people's reaction to your breaking up with Jennifer when you learnt she had MS.'

He didn't answer at first and there was something about the quality of his silence that caused a flicker of fear to touch her heart. Then very quietly he asked, 'And did your parents think that as well?'

She nodded.

'You all thought that of me?' He stared at her and she couldn't fail to see the pain in his eyes.

'What else were we to think?'

He didn't answer, his silence becoming unnerving, and when she examined his features she was dismayed by the bleakness she saw there; then, with almost cold deliberation, he turned away and sat on the edge of the bed with his back to her.

'David, what is it?' she pleaded, disbelieving of the change in him.

His naked back remained straight, unyielding, and without turning he said, 'I'm amazed, that's all. If you thought that, why are you here with me now?'

Without a word, he stood up and began to dress. She watched in silence, her heart crying out to him, suddenly fearful that almost in the same moment that she'd found him she had lost him, but without knowing why.

At last he turned to her and he could not have failed to see the anguish in her eyes. 'David, it doesn't matter; none of it matters now. . .' she began.

'Rachel, I'm sorry, but it does,' he replied tightly. 'There's something I have to do.' Briefly, he touched her face, his strong fingers on her cheek, his thumb beneath her jaw, tilting it upwards.

Then he was gone. The only sounds were his footsteps on the stairs, the slamming of her front door followed by the noise of his car engine as it roared away from her flat.

With a helpless little movement she sat up, drawing up her knees and hugging them as if in some way she might glean comfort from the gesture.

What had gone wrong? What had happened? One moment she had been happier than she'd ever been in her life, the next she was alone again.

She looked round her bedroom and saw that David had left his wristwatch on her bedside table; the scent of the citrus aftershave he used still hung in the air and when finally, in despair, she turned and buried her head in the pillow, the bed beneath her was still warm with the imprint of his body.

# CHAPTER TEN

RACHEL spent a troubled and restless night, her brief snatches of sleep haunted by distressing dreams and the longer periods of wakefulness filled with thoughts and reasonings that chased each other through her mind.

David filled her dreams; the ecstasy of their love-making, and the pain and bewilderment of his abrupt departure. Where had he been going when he left her? What was it he had to do?

Her wakefulness was dogged by growing anxiety over the day ahead; had her mother told Jennifer that David was back in the country, that he worked at OBEX? Had she warned her that there was every possibility they might meet at the Family Day? What would happen if they did meet? How would Jennifer react?

The more the questions tumbled through her brain, the more confused she became. That David's strange behaviour had something to do with Jennifer she had little doubt, so whatever would a meeting between them bring forth? She'd had no chance even to tell David that her family would be at OBEX the following day, so it could be as much a shock for him seeing Jennifer as it would be for her sister.

David had told her to trust him, but had he been

implying that everything would be all right and that their relationship would continue? But if that were the case her parents and Jennifer would still have to be told, as would his mother. Rachel shivered as she visualised the look on Irene Markham's face. And then finally, even if all those problems were surmounted, what of her own feelings?

Really, if she stopped to think, the situation was still the same, nothing had changed. She had little doubt that she had allowed her heart to rule her head, and, much as she had enjoyed what had happened between her and David, could she ultimately trust a man who had treated her sister the way he had? Supposing she, Rachel, had some traumatic happening in her life in the future — would he walk away from her too and again turn his back on his responsibilities?

By the time she got up, after finally falling into a heavy, dreamless sleep just before dawn, Rachel had a headache and felt thoroughly wretched at the thought of what might be to come. Because she wasn't officially on duty she dressed casually in jeans, a white shirt and a long, navy blue knitted coat bright with appliquéd scarlet poppies and peacock butterflies.

An early-morning mist hung over Branchester, the cathedral rising up like some ghostly fairy-tale palace while cobwebs glistened on iron railings and moisture dripped from the branches of the lime trees that fringed the roads.

But by the time Rachel arrived at the factory gates

the October sunshine was doing its best to struggle through with more than a promise of a fine day to come.

The security guard touched his cap, smiled and waved her on, and when she pulled up in the car park she found that in spite of the earliness of the hour some families had already arrived.

Most of the morning would be taken up by employees taking members of their families on tours of the factory, showing them every stage in the production of the Coachliner aircraft which OBEX was renowned for.

In the grounds, beer tents had been erected and caterers brought in to provide coffee, snacks, lunches and other light refreshments. Entertainment would come in the form of the funfair, races and sports for the children, sideshows and tents packed with crafts and fancy merchandise, pleasure flights in light aircraft taking off from the company runway, and then, much later in the evening, the grand firework display that would wind up the day's events.

Rachel wasn't expecting her family to arrive until late morning so she decided on a quick visit to the occupational health centre to see if by any remote chance David might be there.

The shop-floor seemed strangely silent in the absence of the usual sounds of machinery, hammering and drilling and to Rachel's disappointment her own centre was also empty. She decided to while away the time until her family arrived by going through some reports.

When she left the centre a good hour later it was to find dozens of people in little groups strolling around the factory floor and climbing the stairs to the jig platforms. She was about to make her way to the main entrance when a shout halted her.

'Hello, Sister.'

She turned and found Jimmy Warren behind her with a young girl dressed similarly to him in jeans and a leather jacket, her red hair wild and tousled.

'Hello, Jimmy.' She smiled at the girl, who smiled back.

'This is my girlfriend, Stacey,' he said. 'We went to see Len last night,' he added after a pause.

'How was he?' asked Rachel, pleased that Jimmy seemed to have gone to the hospital again of his own accord.

'Not too bad, was he?' He turned to Stacey.

'No, not too bad,' she echoed. 'But it must be terrible to be like that — not to be able to move — or to feel anything.'

'He was talking about that place — Conway House,' said Jimmy.

'How do you think he feels about going there?' asked Rachel.

'Don't know really, it's hard to tell with Len, but he didn't say he didn't want to go, did he, Stace?' He turned to the girl again and she shook her head.

'Well, that's a good start. I expect he was pleased to see you both.'

'Yeah, he was. He didn't think I'd go back. He knows I don't like hospitals.'

'Will you go again, Jimmy?'

'Course we will; Len's my mate. We'll go to Conway House as well when he gets there, won't we?'

Stacey nodded enthusiastically, then they all turned as a minibus pulled up at the main entrance.

'Here comes a party now from Conway House,' said Rachel. 'I must go and help them. Would you like to give a hand with the wheelchairs, Jimmy?'

'Sure, we don't mind.'

They followed her out of the factory and round to the back of the minibus where Sybil and the driver were already helping some of the group to alight. Danny could barely contain himself and was pointing excitedly to the funfair on the spare ground on the far side of the factory.

'Danny's really been looking forward to the fair,' explained Rachel to Jimmy who had pitched in and was helping the driver to lift a wheelchair from the minibus.

Jimmy paused and looked across to the fair. 'It looks as if it's just starting up,' he said as the sound of pop music drifted towards them.

'It would probably be a good time to go now before it gets too crowded.' Rachel turned to Sybil, who was helping Belinda put the strap of her shoulder-bag over her head.

'Well, it would be if David were here,' replied Sybil. 'But I'm not sure what time he'll get here and I don't think Alf and I could manage this lot on our own.'

'We'll give you a hand,' offered Jimmy, glancing at Stacey, who nodded in agreement.

'I'll come as well,' added Rachel.

'I say, that's awfully good of you,' said Sybil gruffly. 'I don't think I could restrain Danny much longer; all he can talk about is driving one of the dodgems.'

The little group set off with Alf and Jimmy pushing wheelchairs and as they approached the funfair Rachel threw Sybil a curious glance. 'Why isn't David here?' She asked the question half fearfully, almost afraid at what she might be about to hear after the event of the previous day.

Sybil's answer, however, was so unexpected it threw her completely.

'It's his mother again,' she said, stopping suddenly to wait for Marjorie, another woman in the group, who was lagging behind.

Rachel too stopped and stared at Sybil. 'His mother?' she asked in amazement.

'Yes, it sounded bad this time. I took his call when he rang in.'

'What sounded bad? I don't understand.'

'Well, his mother, of course. . .' She paused then stared at Rachel. 'Don't you know about it? Hasn't David told you? I thought you would have known.'

'Known what, for heaven's sake? What's this all about?' Rachel, her hands on her hips, half laughing with exasperation, wondered just what demands the formidable Irene Markham was putting on her son.

'His mother has cancer, Rachel,' said Sybil

quietly, and as the smile faded from Rachel's face she added, 'Inoperable cancer; pancreas, I think. Apparently it's only a matter of time.'

'Oh, God!' Rachel's hand flew to her mouth and she stared at Sybil in dismay. 'I had no idea. Why didn't David tell me?'

Sybil shrugged. 'I don't know; maybe he thought the fewer people who knew, the better. I only knew because he's had to change his shifts at Conway House a couple of times so that he could be with her after her chemotherapy sessions.'

They walked on in silence, the music from the fair growing louder as they approached. All Rachel could see in her mind's eye was Irene Markham's gaunt features on the day when she'd gone to Brooklands to pick David up. It was no wonder she'd looked as if she'd aged, she thought guiltily, and no wonder she'd looked miserable; the poor woman didn't have too much to look happy about. She wished David had told her, let her share his pain. All the time she'd been wittering on about Jennifer and her illness, he had kept this to himself, suffering in silence.

'Rachel, will you come on the roundabout with me?' Belinda broke into her thoughts, tugging at her arm to gain her attention. 'I want to ride on a horse.'

Absent-mindedly she stared down at Belinda's happy, shining face. 'What? Oh, yes—yes, of course, Belinda,' she said, dragging herself back to the present.

The carousel, its rows of white horses resplendent

with red leather saddles and black-painted bridles, was thankfully almost empty. They climbed the steps and Rachel helped Belinda to mount one of the horses. For a moment the girl looked afraid and, leaning forward, clung to the horse's neck.

'Will you be all right?' asked Rachel dubiously, worried that Belinda might try to climb from the horse when the carousel was in motion, or, even worse, that she might slip from its back.

'Of course I will.' Belinda threw her a withering look and Rachel smiled back.

'Well, hold on tightly to the pole.' She indicated the gold-painted poles that attached the horses to the roof of the carousel. 'I'll be right here beside you,' she added, climbing on to the next horse.

Belinda waited in growing anticipation, then as the carousel began to move she squealed with excitement and began laughing loudly.

As they moved round, the pace quickening, out of the corner of her eye Rachel saw a little group clustered round the dodgems and Jimmy and Danny climbing into one of the cars, while on the grass below the carousel Sybil stood with the others watching and waving as they whirled past.

The music blared out around them — Beatles songs from the Sixties — and for a brief space of time Rachel forgot her worries and allowed herself to be caught up in Belinda's simple pleasures.

When the carousel eventually slowed to a halt she had difficulty persuading Belinda to get off the horse's back.

'You can have another go later,' she said, taking Belinda's hand and steadying her as she dismounted, 'but there are lots of other things to see; you don't want to spend your money all at once.'

Belinda grumbled but she followed Rachel and they joined the others. For the next hour the fairground gradually filled with people, mainly families with young children or teenagers who had become bored with their tour round the factory and were looking for some excitement. Sideshows did a roaring trade with queues waiting to try their luck on the rifle range, hoop-la, hubbly bubbly or coconut shies. Some went away empty-handed but more often than not a huge cuddly animal was won and before long all the members of the group from Conway House were loaded with prizes.

Loud speakers issued announcements of other entertainments: pleasure flights from the runway, sports attractions including a tug of war and five-a-side football, and a donkey derby in the field behind the car park. The aroma of hotdogs and onions wafted between the tents and mingled with the more pungent smells of engine grease and petrol. Hot air blasted from the generator vehicles but above everything blared the music. Every tent and attraction seemed to be playing something different, and as they wandered round, stepping over lengths of cable, one burst of song would fade only to be instantly replaced by a snatch of something different.

Rachel had stopped to buy candyfloss for her little gang when she saw Belinda waving the yellow fluffy

duck Alf had won on the rifle range towards someone in the crowd. She turned to see who it was and
her heart lurched as David suddenly appeared. He
looked tired and drawn and her heart went out to
him, but when he caught sight of Belinda the smile
was back on his face. Then he turned to Rachel and
for just a moment allowed his gaze to meet hers.

'Hello, David,' said Belinda. 'Have some of this.'
She pulled off a handful of pink candyfloss and
handed it to him. 'It's ever so nice,' she added.

'Thanks, Belinda,' he said solemnly, trying to eat
the fluffly mass even as it began to darken and stick
to his fingers.

'David. . .'

He glanced up and looked at her again and just
for a moment it was as if they were alone in the
midst of the hubbub of the fairground. It was as if
those grey eyes could see into the very depths of her
soul, stirring the desire that lay there waiting to be
aroused, as each of them recalled the passion they
had shared the previous day.

Then she remembered the ending of that interlude
and her pain and bewilderment must have shown in
her eyes because David spoke, but so softly that
only she could hear.

'I must see you later.'

Her breath caught in her throat. Had he done
whatever it was he had to do? Was there, could
there be, a solution to their problems?

'I wanted to phone you but I had no chance. . .'

'Your mother. . .?' she asked swiftly and when

she saw the surprise in his eyes she went on hurriedly, 'Sybil told me.'

'Oh. I wasn't going to say anything.'

'But why? David, why didn't you tell me?' she asked gently. 'Didn't you think I'd understand?'

He was silent for a moment, licking his lips, while in the background the sound of the Beatles blared out. At last, he shrugged. 'No, it wasn't that. I just thought you had enough to be getting on with, what with Jennifer. I didn't want to add to the problems. Besides, there wasn't anything you could do. . . there isn't anything anyone can do. . .' He frowned and she saw a muscle twitch in his jaw.

'Oh, David,' she said softly, placing her hand on his arm, 'I'm so sorry, really I am.'

'Thanks.' He looked at her hand on his arm and said, 'It's life, Rachel. We just have to accept these things and get on with it. Mother's very brave and philosophical about the whole thing; all I can do is make things as easy as possible for her.'

'Is that why you came back from Australia?'

'Of course. At the time I had no other reason to come home, but when I heard my mother only had a short time left it was the only place I wanted to be.'

Suddenly Rachel found she had a lump in her throat. She had been right in her suspicion that David's return had been something to do with a woman, but how wrong she had been over the reason. She blinked and swallowed but before she had time to say more Danny suddenly pushed his way through the crowd, dragging Jimmy behind him.

'Rachel, will you come on the dodgems with me?' A broad grin spread across his features. 'I can drive now, can't I, Jimmy?'

'Yes, mate, you can drive now,' agreed Jimmy.

'All right, Danny,' said Rachel quickly, 'you can drive me.'

'I want a go,' demanded Belinda, trying to wipe the sticky pink mess from her face and hands but only succeeding in making it worse.

'All right, Belinda, I'll drive you,' said David and they all set off across the grass to the dodgem stand.

The music playing on the stand was vintage Shadows and as the guitars belted out 'Apache' David helped Belinda into one of the brightly coloured cars and Rachel followed Danny to another.

A young lad hopped from car to car taking their money, lights sparked and flashed above them and as the cars began to move Belinda's laugh could be heard above the music while Rachel thought Danny would explode with pride as he took the wheel and manoeuvred the little car round the track.

Rachel had always thought that dodgems were inappropriately named, and that day was no exception, for as they cruised round there were many more bumps than dodges, accompanied by screams and shrieks as the guitars throbbed louder than ever and a siren wailed above them,

When it was over and they climbed from the cars Danny needed a considerable amount of calming as his excitement seemed to have reached a peak. David must have anticipated this, for as soon as he left his car he made his way across to them, Belinda in tow with her hand tucked into his arm. 'Come on, Danny, old man,' he said. 'I think it's time we got you something to drink.'

It was as they stepped from the dodgem stand and Rachel turned from helping Belinda down the steep steps to the grass that she saw the little group of her family watching them.

Jennifer, in a blue tracksuit that showed off her blonde hair to perfection, was sitting in her wheelchair. There was a strange expression on her face as she watched Rachel and David.

'Oh!' gasped Rachel, her gaze darting to her father who was standing behind the wheelchair and her mother who stood beside them. 'I didn't know you were here yet.'

'We went to the factory first,' said her father shortly.

'We saw someone called Martin Foulds,' her mother chipped in; 'he said he'd seen you heading in this direction. Hello, David,' she said, then hastily turned to Belinda and Danny. 'Hello, are you having fun?' Her brightness was forced and she was clearly nervous at what might be about to happen.

'This is Belinda and Danny,' explained Rachel by way of introduction. 'They live at Conway House. . .' As she turned she saw that Belinda was bending forward, staring curiously up into Jennifer's face.

'Belinda, this is my sister, Jennifer,' she said.

'Hello, Belinda.' Jennifer smiled. 'Are you enjoying yourself with your friends?'

Belinda nodded. 'Rachel's my friend,' she said solemnly, 'and David's my friend.' Her gaze flickered to David, then, as Jennifer looked up at David and warning bells began to sound in Rachel's head, Belinda said, 'David had a girlfriend called Jennifer, didn't you, David?' then, turning back to Jennifer, she added, 'But Rachel's his girlfriend now.'

# CHAPTER ELEVEN

HER father cleared his throat, her mother looked flustered and Rachel wished the ground would open up and swallow her.

Her gaze flew to Jennifer. Had her sister known David was back in the country, or had it been a shock? Even more worrying, what did Jennifer and her parents think at seeing her with David and at hearing Belinda's announcement?

To her surprise there was a calm, almost bland expression on Jennifer's face, while her parents seemed more embarrassed then shocked. Quickly she turned her head to see David's reaction to seeing his ex-fiancée again after such a long time. Once again, however, she was surprised to find very little response to what she had feared would be an explosive situation as David remained apparently impassive after the initial courtesy greetings.

No one seemed to know what to do next, or what was expected of them, and in the end it was David himself who took control. 'I'm going to take this little gang to get some drinks.' He indicated Danny, Belinda, sublimely oblivious to the possible havoc she might have caused, and the others, who were patiently waiting. Then, turning to Rachel, he added, 'No doubt you'd like to take your family to lunch?'

'What?' Rachel stared blankly at him, then desperately tried to pull herself together. 'Oh, yes — yes, of course,' she agreed as she realised what he was saying.

After taking a somewhat strained parting from David, who said he would see them later, they made their way to one of the refreshment marquees.

Her father bought them a drink and ordered lunch and they wheeled Jennifer's chair up to one of the small tables that had been set up outside the marquee in the sunshine.

'I wish someone would tell me just what's going on.' Ken Stevens sipped his pint, then, setting his glass on the table, looked indignantly from his wife to his daughters.

'Not now, Ken.' Valerie Stevens appeared uncomfortable and on edge.

'What do you mean, not now?' He looked affronted. 'I think I'm entitled to an explanation.'

Rachel stared at the ground and wished they'd all go home, but when her father spoke again she looked up in surprise.

'I still don't know what happened last night, when Markham came round. What did he want, for God's sake?'

'What do you mean?' Rachel looked up quickly but before her father could explain further Jennifer intervened, manoeuvring her chair closer to the table.

'Dad, if you don't mind, I'd like to speak to Rachel alone about that.'

'There you go — more secrets. I'm the last to know anything around here.' Ken Stevens was clearly exasperated.

'No, you're not,' his wife broke in. 'I don't know what's going on either, but I'm sure the girls will tell us when they're ready. Ah, here comes our lunch.' She looked up as a waitress appeared carrying a tray loaded with plates of crusty bread, cheese and pickles. She was silent while the girl unloaded the tray then when they were alone again she shook out her serviette, glanced round at the others and said, 'When we've had our lunch, Ken, you can take me to watch the donkey derby and we'll leave these two to talk.'

Her husband grunted but Valerie Stevens then skilfully changed the subject, asking Rachel questions about the factory and the Coachliner aircraft and finally bringing the conversation round to the group from Conway House.

'They certainly seemed to be enjoying themselves,' she said; 'you'd have thought that young man Danny had just won a Grand Prix instead of driving round a dodgem track.'

'It would have felt like that to Danny,' said Rachel. 'He was so proud to have actually been able to drive me round himself.'

'Did you say they live at Conway House?' asked Jennifer.

'That particular group do,' said Rachel, and found herself wondering if that was what David had visited her family for — to discuss the possibility of Jennifer going to Conway House. It had to be something like that. What other reason could he have had? A sudden wave of panic swept over her and she glanced at the others but it didn't seem as if she was going to learn anything for the moment.

After they'd finished their lunch Valerie Stevens took her husband off across the field to where a little knot of donkeys were assembling to take part in the donkey derby, an important annual event at the OBEX Family Day.

As they watched their parents go it was Rachel who spoke first. 'I'm sorry, Jennifer, about what Belinda said. I wouldn't have had that happen for anything.'

'It's all right, you don't have to apologise.' A tight little smile played around Jennifer's mouth. 'Besides, poor Belinda couldn't have known the situation, could she?'

Rachel shook her head then looked at her sister curiously. 'I'm not sure I know the situation, let alone Belinda,' she said. Frowning, she added, 'What did Dad mean about David going to the house last night?'

'There's no mystery about it; David did come to the house. He came to see me.'

Rachel stiffened and waited then when Jennifer made no attempt at further explanation she said, 'Was it to do with your MS?'

Her sister took a sip of her drink before answering. 'That was mentioned, certainly, but it wasn't the reason David wanted to see me.' She shook back her long blonde hair.

Rachel thought how lovely she looked, then found herself wondering just what had happened the previous night between her sister and David—a couple who had once meant the world to each other. She tried to dismiss the thought even as it formed. 'I don't understand,' she said at last. 'What did David want?'

Jennifer was silent again as if choosing her words with great care, then slowly she said, 'Before I answer that, Rachel, there's something I want to ask you.' She paused only fractionally before saying, 'Are you in love with David?'

Rachel drew in her breath sharply. How should she answer? How would Jennifer react if she admitted she loved David? Would she be hurt or would she warn her against him?

While she was still floundering for a reply, Jennifer leaned forward and touched her arm. 'It's all right,' she said quietly. 'You don't need to answer. It's right there on your face.'

Rachel lowered her gaze. 'Yes,' she admitted at last. 'I am in love with him.' Then, glancing up again quickly, a troubled look in her green eyes, she added, 'But I didn't want to hurt you, Jennifer, honestly; that was the last thing I wanted.'

'Why should you hurt me?'

'Well, you and David. . .you loved him. . .' She trailed off, confused by the amused look of surprise on her sister's face. Then when Jennifer didn't reply she muttered, 'Damn it, Jen, you were engaged to him.'

'It was a long time ago, Rachel.' The smile slowly faded from Jennifer's face and she sighed, then a far-away look came into her eyes as she added, 'A lot's happened since then.'

'That's true,' agreed Rachel, 'and what's happened hasn't exactly been a bundle of fun for you. But at the time you were heartbroken when David left you. I was there, remember? You can't pretend otherwise now.' She looked at her sister, who had grown very still and was staring down at her hands.

'I was heartbroken, certainly,' Jennifer agreed softly at last, 'but it wasn't over David leaving.'

Rachel stared at her. 'What do you mean?'

At first Jennifer remained silent, as if she was fighting some immense inner struggle, then quietly she began to explain. 'I was heartbroken when I found I had MS: it seemed the end of all my hopes and dreams, of my career and possibly of marrying and having children.' She hesitated and her fingers began pleating a paper serviette that lay on the table; then, glancing briefly at Rachel and taking a deep breath, she continued, 'But I was heartbroken over something else as well, and it wasn't David. It just seemed easier to let everyone assume that at the time. . .' She trailed off.

'Jennifer, what are you talking about?' Rachel leaned forward, frowning, almost oblivious to the crowds of people who were milling round them looking for tables. 'None of this is making sense.'

'It's simple really,' Jennifer went on at last. 'Everyone thought David broke off the engagement, but the truth of the matter was it was me who ended it.'

'You?' Rachel sat back in her chair in bewilderment. 'But why?' Then, her eyes widening, she nodded and said, 'Oh, I see, it was because of your MS. You didn't think it was fair to David. Was that it?'

'No, Rachel, that wasn't it.' Jennifer shook her head. 'I'm not that noble!' She gave a short, derisive laugh. 'I broke my engagement to David Markham because I was in love with someone else.'

Rachel stared at her sister in silent astonishment.

'It's true. Don't look so surprised, these things do happen.'

'I know. . .it's just that. . .' Rachel shrugged helplessly, then, still bewildered, asked, 'Who was it, for heaven's sake?'

'Paul Mason,' Jennifer answered flatly and there was no trace of emotion in her voice.

'Paul Mason?' Rachel stared wildly at her as an image of the gynae registrar at St Clare's came into her mind—an image of a stocky, balding man approaching middle age; then, as another thought struck her, she said, 'But. . .but. . .he was. . .'

'Married? Yes, he was. He was married to Sonia at the time.'

'At the time. . .?'

'They're divorced now, apparently, and Paul's married to someone else, but at the time he was going to divorce Sonia and marry me. That's when I broke things off with David.'

Rachel stared at her sister in silence, shocked by what she had just heard, not so much by the fact that Paul Mason had been married but because he was as different from David Markham as it was possible for a man to be, and none of them had even suspected what had been happening. As yet another thought entered her head she frowned again. 'Was all this before your MS was diagnosed?' she asked slowly.

'Oh, yes.' Jennifer nodded, and there was a tight little smile on her face.

'But why didn't you say anything? Why didn't you tell any of us?'

'Cowardice, I suppose.' She shrugged. 'I was leading up to it slowly. You know how Dad is about these things. I was dreading telling him. Anyway, before I got round to it, my symptoms started and shortly afterwards, as you know, MS was diagnosed.'

'What happened then?'

'Paul told me it was all over between us; that it would never work out and that he and Sonia were going to make a fresh start. But the real reason, I knew, was because he couldn't face up to my being ill. Soon after, he and Sonia moved down south.'

'So it wasn't David who couldn't face up to your illness at all?'

'No, it wasn't David.' Jennifer gave a rueful smile. 'David would have stood by me. I know that; he was made of stronger stuff than Paul. But by that time, of course, it was well and truly over between us and he'd left for Australia.'

'Do you wish you'd stayed with him?' She said it quietly, half fearfully, and was relieved when Jennifer shook her head.

'No, in spite of what you might think. One thing I did learn from loving Paul was that I wasn't in love with David. It would have been wrong to marry him; he deserves better.'

'But why did you let us all go on thinking that David had left you?'

Jennifer shrugged. 'It was wrong, I know, but, as I said, it was easier than trying to explain about Paul, and, to be perfectly honest, no one ever mentioned David to me after he'd gone. I suppose they were all afraid of upsetting me. In the end, I simply let them go on thinking what they wanted to think.'

'Until now,' said Rachel quietly.

'Yes, until now,' agreed her sister.

'Did you know David was back in the country?'

'Yes, Mum told me a couple of days go, and that he was working at OBEX. I was surprised, certainly, but I didn't think it would affect me too much.' She paused then smiled at Rachel. 'Until last night, when David came to see me.'

'So why did he go to see you? It must have been quite a shock when he turned up on the doorstep.'

'It was,' Jennifer admitted, then added, 'until I understood why. He said he'd come to ask me if I would be prepared to explain to you what had

happened five years ago.. When I asked him why he
wanted me to do that, he said it was because he was
in love with you.'

Rachel stared at Jennifer and her heart gave a
great lurch as what her sister had just said began to
sink in, then she frowned. 'But why didn't David
just tell me himself?'

'You'll have to ask him that, but my guess is that
he was too much of a gentleman. He must have
realised you didn't know about Paul and he wasn't
prepared to blacken my name in any way.' She
paused, and when she looked up her eyes were
suspiciously bright. 'He's a great guy, you know,
Rachel.'

She nodded, unexpectedly lost for words, and
they both sat in silence.

Then all at once Rachel had to fight a sudden
impulse to go and find David, for at that moment all
she wanted was once more to feel the strength of his
arms around her. Instead she and Jennifer absent-
mindedly watched aircraft taking off and landing on
the company runway, then another thought suddenly
struck her and she said, 'Do you know why he came
back from Australia?'

'I asked him that last night,' admitted Jennifer. 'I
couldn't understand why he'd given up a job he
clearly loved to come back here.'

'And did he tell you?'

'Yes, although very reluctantly. He said his
mother is critically ill.' She gave Rachel a questioning glance. 'What is it, cancer?'

Rachel nodded. 'Yes, apparently she only has a short time to live; David came back to be with her — he's even living at Brooklands.'

'Poor Irene, and poor David; he's going to need a lot of support in the weeks to come.' Then impulsively she added, 'I'm glad he has you, Rachel.'

'And you really don't mind?' She threw her sister an apprehensive glance but was reassured to see she was smiling.

'Of course I don't mind. Oh, I confess to feeling a pang when I first saw David again — I wouldn't be human if I hadn't — but, as I said before, it was over between us a very long time ago, probably even before I fell for Paul if the truth be known.'

'I've been so worried about you finding out,' admitted Rachel, and already the relief was apparent in her tone. 'I was so afraid you would be hurt, then I found myself wondering if I could trust David or whether he would walk out on me at the first sign of trouble.'

'Well, you can put your mind at rest on both those counts now.'

In the distance the girls could see their parents returning across the field. 'I can't say I was exactly looking forward to telling them either,' said Rachel.

'Don't worry about that. Leave the parents to me; I'll do any necessary explaining,' said Jennifer, then paused as a loudspeaker announcement suddenly echoed across the field.

'Would all emergency and medical staff please report to the main entrance of the factory? We have a red-alert situation. Would all emergency and medical staff please. . .?'

'I say, Rachel, does that mean you?' Startled, Jennifer looked up but Rachel was already on her feet.

'It does. Will you be OK, Jen? Mum and Dad are almost here.'

'Just go!'

Rachel paused for one second, long enough to squeeze her sister's hand in a gesture that spoke volumes, then she sped away back towards the factory.

She arrived at the same moment as Nina and they saw that Greg was already unlocking the factory ambulance and David was in consultation with one of the factory managers.

'What is it?' gasped Nina, out of breath from running.

'A pilot of a ten-seater has radioed in to say he's having undercarriage problems,' explained the manager. 'He's circling again but if the undercarriage fails it looks as if he may have to make a crash landing. He wants our emergency crews in position with county back-up. I've alerted the county fire and ambulance services and the police.'

'Right.' David glanced round. Briefly his gaze rested on Rachel and she saw the flicker of uncertainty in his eyes but there was no time for questions. 'Looks as if we're all here,' he said, 'so let's go.'

They climbed into the ambulance, David in the front with Greg, and Rachel and Nina in the back, and within minutes they were hurtling towards the company airfield accompanied by the two factory fire engines and the security vehicles.

Their progress was hampered by the vast crowds and the cars that thronged what would normally have been a clear area but people soon scattered from their path as with lights flashing and sirens wailing they forged ahead.

On the edge of the runway Greg brought the ambulance to a halt and while they prepared to wait for the incoming aircraft, David maintained radio contact with the control tower.

To add to the difficulties, pleasure flights were still in progress and, while it had been relatively easy to prevent any more from taking off after hearing of the emergency situation, it had also been necessary to radio to others to stay in the air and not attempt to land until the crisis was over.

'Who exactly is in this aircraft?' asked Rachel as they waited, the tension mounting. 'Were they coming here anyway or are they just using the runway?'

'Oh, they were coming here all right,' replied David grimly. 'Would you believe it's no less than some of the company directors and their wives paying a visit to Family Day?'

'Crikey, that's all we need,' said Greg with a groan. 'Make sure you get this right, you guys, or we could all be in the dole queue on Monday.' For once his joking did nothing to ease the tension and no one laughed.

Seconds later sunlight flashed on metal and the aircraft appeared in the skies above them. The control tower confirmed that the pilot was going to attempt to land and that the aircraft's undercarriage was indeed jammed.

Rachel leaned forward between the front seats of the ambulance and as she glanced down she saw that David's knuckles showed white as he gripped his black case, his other hand on the door catch, ready to run; Greg was gnawing the side of his thumb and behind her Nina was breathing deeply. Her own nerves were stretched to breaking-point and she couldn't allow herself even to contemplate the changes that would now come in her relationship with David; that luxury would come later, because for the moment lives were in danger. Instead, she watched through the ambulance windscreen, her heart in her mouth as the plane lost height and approached the runway.

It touched the ground at what appeared to be an impossible speed and skidded terrifyingly along the runway amid clouds of dust accompanied by a scraping, nerve-shattering, high-pitched screech.

'It's overshot the runway,' shouted Greg as the plane bumped sickeningly across the field and finally slithered to a halt in the long grass on the far perimeters of the airfield.

'We're on our way,' reported David into the radio as Greg shot the ambulance into gear, let out the clutch and accelerated away across the field.

They arrived at the aircraft at the same instant as

the factory fire crew. The fire officer took command, organising the immediate covering of the aircraft with foam in an attempt to prevent it bursting into flames.

The aircraft was so silent, the atmosphere so eerie that as the medical team jumped from the ambulance they all began to fear the worst for the passengers inside — that they might not have survived the shock and impact of the crash landing.

Then to everyone's relief the emergency door was suddenly opened from the inside and a man appeared. His face was chalk-white and wore a dazed expression, and the uniform he was wearing was crumpled and torn but thankfully he didn't appear to be badly injured.

'We have casualties in here.' His voice was croaked and hoarse and his shocked stare came to rest on David as if he instinctively knew he was a doctor.

'We're right behind you,' called David, indicating for Rachel and Nina to accompany him and telling Greg to bring the oxygen cylinder from the ambulance.

The interior of the stricken aircraft was chaotic, with the passengers' belongings strewn around clogging the gangway. The atmosphere was heavy, oppressive, the smell not immediately identifiable but a combination of human and engine smells, while the only sounds were a soft moaning from a woman towards the front of the plane and the voice of a man trying to reassure someone.

The man who had opened the emergency door identified himself as the co-pilot and informed them that the pilot who had been at the controls had been knocked unconscious at the moment of impact and was badly injured.

'We have eight passengers,' he went on, 'two women and six men.'

'Let's get injuries assessed,' said David. 'County ambulances are on their way, but we'll do any first aid we can.'

While David and Greg made their way to the front of the plane, Rachel and Nina attempted to assess the condition of the passengers who had been seated at the rear. All were still fastened into their safety belts and some were still in the position that the pilot had obviously instructed them to adopt, leaning forward with their arms over their heads.

Swiftly Rachel and Nina moved from person to person, releasing seatbelts, offering reassurance and assessing injuries. One woman appeared to be suffering from severe whiplash injury and Nina, no doubt mindful of Len Seager, hurried back to the ambulance for a neck collar to immobilise her.

The impact of the landing had pushed one man forward under his seatbelt and his legs were trapped beneath the seat in front. Blood was seeping rapidly through his trousers and Rachel had just attempted to staunch the flow when she felt someone touch her shoulder.

'Sister, I believe this gentleman is having an

angina attack.' The voice was quiet, cultured and free from panic.

Rachel looked over her shoulder and saw a tall, white-haired man in a crumpled dark suit. He had a cut on his forehead and blood was trickling down his face. He was pointing to a large man on the other side of the gangway who was slumped back in his seat clutching his chest; his face was grey and his forehead beaded with perspiration.

Swiftly Rachel glanced round but there was no sign of Nina yet. David and Greg were still at the front of the plane, so, beckoning to the white-haired man, she said, 'Would you please come here and keep up pressure on this man's leg? He's bleeding heavily.'

He nodded and took Rachel's place while she crawled forward into the space beside the other man.

To her relief, although it was very faint, she found a pulse, and quickly she loosened his tie, unbuttoned his shirt and somehow manoeuvred him into a better position, all the while talking to him, reassuring him, telling him he was safe.

Then she began to make her way down the plane to find Greg, who had oxygen, and David, who would have glyceryl trinitrate in his case.

Greg was assisting the woman they had heard moaning and who looked as if she'd dislocated her jaw while David was with the pilot. One glance told Rachel the pilot had sustained serious chest injuries.

Briefly she told David what she wanted and he

nodded towards his open case. 'There's a glyceryl trinitrate aerosol in there; take that,' he instructed briefly.

And it was then, in the midst of the suffering and chaos round them, as Rachel knelt on the ground and took from David's case the aerosol that would hopefully save a man's life, that he suddenly looked across at her.

For one unbelievable moment their eyes met and once again it was as if they had stepped back into their own circle of magic. Then Rachel remembered that Jennifer had said that David had told her he was in love with her and in that moment she knew that what her sister had said had been the truth, because it was there in his eyes.

# CHAPTER TWELVE

MOMENTS later Rachel was beside the patient again, where she administered the antianginal medication spray beneath his tongue, then, closing his mouth, put the oxygen mask over his nose to assist his breathing.

Seconds later the police, county ambulance and fire crews arrived and the process of transporting the passengers to the ambulances began.

The most seriously injured were the pilot, who had a crushed thorax and whose lung had been pierced by one of his ribs, the man with his legs trapped, and the woman with spinal injuries. The remainder, with the exception of the woman with the dislocated jaw and the man with the angina attack, were mainly suffering from severe shock and were quickly taken out to the ambulances.

When the angina patient seemed to be stable he too was transported to an ambulance to be taken to hospital so that he could rest and fully recover from his attack.

After a long struggle David and Greg managed to extricate the pilot from the tangled control panel and administered oxygen to help his breathing; then together, with help from the paramedics, they transferred him to a stretcher.

The fire crew had to cut free the man with his legs trapped, after Rachel and Nina had set up an intravenous infusion and David had given him a pethidine injection to help control his pain. The metal supports of the seat in front had cut deeply into his legs, revealing his shattered shin-bones. Rachel and the white-haired man sat with him, each holding one of his hands in an effort to calm him.

At last when the man's legs were freed and he too was carried out to the waiting ambulance, Rachel stood up and flexed her cramped muscles. Looking down at the man who had quietly assisted her and whose clothes were now covered in the other man's blood, she said, 'You'd better go with them as well.'

'I don't think there's any need for that,' he replied. 'I'm perfectly all right.'

'Even so, you've had a severe shock and you've had a bang on your head.' She pointed to his forehead where the blood had congealed and dried around the cut. 'You should go to the hospital for a check-up,' she added firmly.

'Very well, if you insist,' he replied, then, turning to David, he said, 'I must compliment you all on your efficiency and your bravery here today.' And, with a little nod, he followed one of the paramedics out to join the co-pilot in the last of the ambulances.

'Nice chap,' said Greg as he began clearing up their equipment.

'Yes,' agreed Rachel. 'He was a tremendous help too.' Then, glancing at David, she said, 'You do know who he was?'

David shook his head.

'Sir Anthony Fellowes, the OBEX chairman.'

David raised his eyebrows. 'I didn't know; he hasn't been to the factory since I've been here.'

'I shouldn't think he'd forget this visit in a hurry,' muttered Greg.

'No,' agreed Nina as they climbed wearily from the aircraft and back into their ambulance, 'that was the real thing this time, certainly no casualty-faking.'

'I wonder what Ron Banks at Health and Safety will make of it?' Rachel smiled.

'I expect he timed the whole thing with a stop-watch,' said Greg. 'He's probably waiting to tell us we were a tenth of a second late.'

They all laughed and it helped to relieve the tension, but when they returned to the occupational health centre, far from being criticised for their performance, they heard only praise and found they were being treated as heroes.

Rachel had imagined that the accident would put paid to Family Day and that the other activities, including the firework display, would be cancelled, but within the hour a message came through from the hospital from Sir Anthony to say that, because miraculously there had been no fatalities, with even the pilot surviving his injuries, it was his express wish that the Family Day celebration should continue.

While they cleaned up and packed their equipment away Nina put the kettle on and made tea, then they all collapsed in the staff-room.

'Do you know, it's five o'clock!' Nina said as she handed round steaming mugs. 'I hadn't realised it had all taken so long—it was lunchtime when the alarm went off.'

'It was getting that poor man free that took the time,' said Rachel. 'I really feared for his legs at one point.'

'They still may have to amputate,' said David quietly.

They fell silent, each reflecting on what had happened, then, suddenly changing the subject, Nina said, 'Was that your sister I saw you talking to earlier, Rachel?'

She nodded. 'Yes, that was Jennifer, and my parents.'

'Oh, I didn't see your parents,' Nina replied quickly. 'When I saw you it was just the pair of you. You were sitting outside the marquee deep in conversation. In fact, you were so engrossed I passed right by and you didn't even look up when I spoke.'

'Oh, Nina, I'm sorry,' said Rachel, then, seeing Nina's quizzical look, she added, 'Yes, we were pretty engrossed. . .there was something we needed to discuss. . .' She trailed off and, feeling her cheeks redden, she glanced up to find David's eyes on her. He was sprawled in an armchair opposite and the expression on his face clearly told her that he knew exactly what she and Jennifer had been discussing.

'Will your family still be here?' asked Nina, glancing from Rachel to David and back to Rachel again, a slightly bemused look on her face as if she didn't really understand what was happening between them but wished she did.

'I shouldn't think so; Jennifer will have had enough by now.'

'Are you all staying for the fireworks?' asked Greg.

'I think I'll go home for a couple of hours then come back later,' replied Nina, standing up and draining her mug.

'Good idea,' replied Rachel. 'I'll do the same.'

David stood up then and held the door open, and as Greg and Nina left the room he turned to Rachel. 'I'll run you home; you can leave your car here until later.'

He said it lightly but as she followed him from the staff-room she was aware that her heart had begun to beat very fast.

They drove in silence for a while, with Rachel content just to be beside him, happy in the knowledge that all their difficulties had somehow been resolved. But there were still things that needed to be said, explanations to be given, and in the end it was David who broke the silence.

'From your conversation with Nina, can I assume that Jennifer told you why I visited her last night?' He threw her a quick glance, briefly taking his eyes from the road.

'Yes, David, she did.'

'Were you shocked at what she told you?'

She hesitated. 'Yes,' she admitted slowly at last,

'I suppose I was shocked. . .the truth was very different from what I'd imagined.'

'So I'm not the bad guy any more?' He grinned suddenly, making him look boyish.

'I never. . .' she floundered, not knowing quite what to say.

'Oh, yes, you did,' he interrupted. 'From the moment I walked into OBEX it was plainly written all over your face. You didn't like me. I wasn't too sure why at first. I seemed to recall that in the past when we'd met we'd got on reasonably well, so I assumed that it must have been something that Jennifer had told you that had turned you against me, or, failing that, that you were just embarrassed at having to work with your sister's ex-fiancé.'

'Wasn't that understandable?'

'Not really. Remember, I assumed you knew it was Jennifer who had broken off the engagement and the reason she did so.'

'So when did you suspect otherwise?'

'When you said something about the real tragedy for anyone facing a handicap is when expected support is withdrawn, then yesterday at your flat I realised that you thought I'd walked out on Jennifer when I discovered she had MS. Suddenly, it all made sense,' he added as he brought the car to a halt in front of her flat.

'We knew nothing about Paul Mason or Jennifer's involvement with him,' said Rachel slowly. 'It seems terrible now, David, to think that you've taken the blame for so long for something you didn't do. Not that it was ever even mentioned,' she added hurriedly; 'Jennifer just never offered any explanation and we all jumped to our own conclusions. Heaven knows what you must think of us.'

'I must confess I'm pretty sick about it all,' he said seriously, then when she threw him a startled glance he suddenly grinned. 'I would think, however, that, provided you're prepared to make amends, I could overlook your attitude towards me.' Leaning forward, he suddenly tilted her face towards him and in the same movement covered her lips with his.

When some minutes later he drew away, he said softly, 'And I'd say those amends could start now, with you asking me in. After all, we have a good couple of hours before we have to go back.'

Rachel got out of the car and with a little ripple of laughter led the way into her flat.

The evening shadows were lengthening, one or two lights were coming on in buildings across the city and the dark mass of the cathedral stood out sharply against the soft viridian sky.

They stood, their arms round each other, staring at the view before them, then at last, turning from the window, David sat on the bed and pulled her between his legs so that as she stood with her hands on his shoulders he pressed his head against her stomach.

For a long moment he held her tightly against him as if he was afraid she might try to elude him, then when he seemed sure of her his hands encircled her waist, moulded her hips and moved upwards, unbuttoning her shirt, pulling it from the waistband of her jeans, then slipping it from her shoulders until it fell to the floor. Lightly he brushed her breasts with his lips, at the same time cupping them, gently caressing with his thumbs until her nipples ached with desire.

She leaned forward, her hair falling across her face, and as he lifted his head she brought her lips down on his, parting them with her tongue at the same moment as she felt his hands unzipping her jeans.

He had been remarkably restrained until then, but when she felt him ease her jeans down over her hips she suddenly caught his sense of urgency as, with a low groan, he roughly pulled her even closer, burying his head against the soft skin of her thighs. She threw back her head, arching her back, straining her body even closer against him.

After that all pretence at restraint was gone as David swiftly undressed then reached out and pulled her down on to him. With a gasp that turned to a shuddering sigh, she felt their flesh merge.

A moment of stillness, of sweet realisation followed. Then, as he stirred, her body came alive and at last, matching the rhythm of his, she once more gave herself up to the unashamed pleasure of loving and being loved by him.

Afterwards, their passion temporarily spent, they lay in each other's arms watching the sky darken above the city, both busy with their own thoughts. It was David who moved first, running his finger down the length of her profile.

'What are you thinking?' he asked lazily.

'Hmm?' She shifted slightly, her body still warm from his.

'You seemed deep in thought.'

'I was.'

'So are you going to tell me?' There was a trace of amusement now in the softness of his tone.

'I was thinking about the day I went to your house to pick you up.'

'What about it?' He turned slightly towards her, resting his weight on his elbow so that he could see her face, watch her lips as she spoke.

'It was your mother.'

'What about my mother?' Just for a second she thought she detected a wary note in his voice.

'She didn't seem particularly pleased to see me.'

'You have to excuse her at the moment; she. . .'

'Oh, I know she's ill, David, please, I didn't mean that; I know she wouldn't exactly be on top of the world. No, what I meant was, it was me in particular she wasn't happy to see.'

He didn't answer immediately and in the half-light she tried to examine his features. 'Did she know? About Jennifer, I mean?'

Still he hesitated, then, lowering his head, he said, 'Yes, she knew, Rachel. She was the one person I told. She came to my flat the night I found Jennifer with Mason.'

Her eyes widened in surprised. 'You actually found them together?'

'Didn't Jennifer tell you that?'

'No, she simply said she broke off the engagement because she was in love with him.'

He shrugged. 'Well, that was true, I suppose, but it was after I found them together in her flat. I went there unexpectedly as a surprise; she thought I was on duty—they were in bed. . .'

'Oh, David.' Reaching out, she touched his face and he turned and kissed the tips of her fingers.

'I went home and just after I got in my mother phoned; she must have known from my voice that something was wrong. She drove round straight away and it all came out.'

'Had it been a total shock to you or had you suspected anything?'

'At the time it was a shock, but afterwards when I looked back the signs had been there. Jennifer had been restless and we hadn't been getting on very well. Even I had come to realise we weren't as compatible as I'd thought we were. Anyway, Jennifer phoned the next morning and told me it was all over. Soon after that I made arrangements to go to Australia; I just felt I didn't want to be around when Mason and Jennifer got together. Then just before I left I heard that Jennifer's MS had been diagnosed. But I wasn't aware that Mason had left her.'

'Would you still have gone, if you had known?' Rachel found herself holding her breath as she waited for his answer.

'Yes, I would. By then our love was dead. It died for me the moment I found Mason in her bed.'

They fell silent, each reflecting on what was past, then slowly Rachel said, 'It was no wonder your mother wasn't too pleased to see me. She knew how badly one sister had treated you; she quite obviously didn't want to see you become associated with the other. . .'

'And your parents quite obviously hate my guts because they think I walked out on Jennifer when she most needed me. . . My God! What a mess!'

'Well, hopefully, it'll all be sorted out by now; Jennifer was going to explain everything at home.'

'And I've told my mother I'm in love with you.'

'Good heavens, what did she say to that?'

'She just wants to see me happy before. . .' He trailed off then took a deep breath. 'You know what mothers are,' he shrugged, then, looking at Rachel searchingly, he added, 'The future may not be easy for us.'

'As long as I'm with you, I can face anything,' she said simply.

'That's how I feel.'

He drew her close again and they fell silent, Rachel reflecting on how hard it must have been for David not to have told her what had really happened between himself and her sister, then another thought struck her. 'Will you want to go back to Australia eventually?'

'I don't know. I certainly enjoyed the life out there. When I first came home I thought I would stay with my mother as long as she needed me, then I would go back. Now I'm not so sure. I actually enjoy working at OBEX; it's a lot more varied than I ever imagined. Take today, for instance. . .'

'Don't count on too many incidents like that,' she laughed.

'No, maybe not, but even the routine work is interesting; I've enjoyed the accident prevention side of things and I've come to realise the value of our chat-line; then, of course, there's my work at Conway House and I've become totally involved with that. Which reminds me. . .' He paused and chuckled. 'Tomorrow we must go and see Belinda. I think she should be the first to know that you are now officially my girlfriend.'

They both laughed then Rachel said, 'Talking of Conway House, did you mention anything to Jennifer?' Suddenly she was curious as to what her sister's reaction might have been.

'I did.' He smiled.

'And?'

'She was all for it, believe it or not. In fact, she had been thinking along those lines herself. She said she'd realised how tired your parents were becoming and she knew that if she wanted to remain at home on a long-term basis she would have to have some form of respite care. I suggested she get your father to bring her along to the Rosemount wing in the next day or so, so she can see for herself.'

'So things really do seem to be sorting themselves out, don't they?' said Rachel, a touch of surprise in her tone.

'There is just one thing.'

'Oh?'

'We've discussed what just about everyone wants, except you.'

'What do you mean?' She looked startled for a moment.

'Well, how would you feel if at some point in the future I said I wanted to go back to Australia?'

'I would go with you.'

'And if I decided to stay here?'

'Then I stay here.' She stared into his eyes, those steady grey eyes that so fascinated her. 'It's quite simple, really, David—I love you, and where you are is where I want to be. Don't you believe me?'

His breath caught in his throat and he cupped her face in his hands, his fingers becoming entangled in her hair while urgently his gaze searched her face. 'Oh, yes,' he murmured. 'You even loved me when you thought the worst of me, didn't you?'

'Yes, David, I did,' she admitted.

'And I loved you from the moment I walked into the factory, even if you did have a false impression of me. I think,' he said, moving slightly so that his body covered hers again, 'that we have a lot of lost time to make up for.'

'When do you suggest we start?' she whispered.

'I always say there's no time like the present.'

Rachel, lifting her face for his kiss, didn't feel inclined to argue.

# FREE
## GOLD PLATED BRACELET

Mills & Boon would like to give you something extra special this Mother's Day—a Gold Plated Bracelet absolutely *FREE* when you purchase a 'Happy Mother's Day' pack.

The pack features 4 new Romances by popular authors—Victoria Gordon, Debbie Macomber, Joanna Neil and Anne Weale.

Mail-away offer —
see pack for details.
Offer closes 31.5.94

Available now

Price £7.20

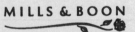

# LOVE ON CALL
# 4 FREE BOOKS AND 2 FREE GIFTS
## FROM MILLS & BOON

Capture all the drama and emotion of a hectic medical world when you accept 4 Love on Call romances PLUS a cuddly teddy bear and a mystery gift - absolutely FREE and without obligation. And, if you choose, go on to enjoy 4 exciting Love on Call romances every month for only £1.80 each! Be sure to return the coupon below today to: Mills & Boon Reader Service, FREEPOST, PO Box 236, Croydon, Surrey CR9 9EL.

— — — — — — **NO STAMP REQUIRED** — — — — —

**YES!** Please rush me 4 FREE Love on Call books and 2 FREE gifts! Please also reserve me a Reader Service subscription, which means I can look forward to receiving 4 brand new Love on Call books for only £7.20 every month, postage and packing FREE. If I choose not to subscribe, I shall write to you within 10 days and still keep my FREE books and gifts. I may cancel or suspend my subscription at any time. I am over 18 years. Please write in BLOCK CAPITALS.

Ms/Mrs/Miss/Mr _____ **EP63D**

Address _____

_____

Postcode _____ Signature _____

Offer closes 31st March 1994. The right is reserved to refuse an application and change the terms of this offer. One application per household. Offer not valid to current Love on Call subscribers. Offer valid only in UK and Eire. Overseas readers please write for details. Southern Africa write to IBS, Private Bag, X3010, Randburg, 2125, South Africa. You may be mailed with offers from other reputable companies as a result of this application. Please tick box if you would prefer not to receive such offers ☐

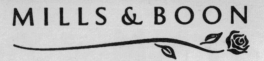

# LOVE ON CALL

The books for enjoyment this month are:

**SURGEON'S DILEMMA** Margaret Barker
**A LOVING LEGACY** Marion Lennox
**FALSE IMPRESSIONS** Laura MacDonald
**NEVER PAST LOVING** Margaret O'Neill

❤     ❤     ❤     ❤     ❤

## Treats in store!

Watch next month for the following absorbing stories:

**PICKING UP THE PIECES** Caroline Anderson
**IN THE HEAT OF THE SUN** Jenny Ashe
**LEGACY OF SHADOWS** Marion Lennox
**LONG HOT SUMMER** Margaret O'Neill